#3
V
FIRST

Untimely

Death

By Cyril Hare

SUICIDE EXCEPTED
UNTIMELY DEATH

Untimely

Death

CYRIL HARE

New York 1958

THE MACMILLAN COMPANY

To
MICHAEL GILBERT

Note

Exmoor, where the action of this book is represented as occurring, is, thank heaven, a real place, inhabited by living men and women. It should therefore be made clear beyond the possibility of doubt that the localities and characters here depicted are purely imaginary and bear no relation whatever to any existing place or person.

C.H.

Contents

CHAPTER I

Journey into the Past

The holiday had been Eleanor's idea in the first place. Holidays for Francis Pettigrew signified first and foremost strange beds and a strange bed meant, for the first night at least, waking up in the small hours instead of sleeping through till dawn. None the less, as he lay wakefully watching the shifting pattern of the moonshadows on the wall, he was prepared to concede that it was an excellent idea. Nowadays, he acknowledged, not without shame, it would be difficult to find any departure from the monotony of their rather humdrum joint existence that was not due to an idea of Eleanor's. More and more, with advancing years, he had tended to resign the initiative in affairs to his still young wife. It made for peace, and so far he had had no reason to regret it.

It had been Eleanor's idea, to begin with, to sell half her slender store of gilt-edged securities and invest them in industrial shares just at the beginning of the Stock Exchange boom in the early nineteen-fifties. It had been her idea, again, to convert part of the resulting profits into a small car, a moment before the prices of her holdings began to slide downwards in 1955. From

9

the acquisition of the car to going away for a holiday was no more than a step. But it was a step that had consumed rather more time in the taking than either of them had contemplated. Eleanor had carried out her financial transactions with a gay disregard for the head-shaking of experts that had been triumphantly justified by the result. There are, however, some matters in which the head-shaking of experts is apt to be decisive, and the driving test is one of them. There had been a period when the whole project seemed likely to founder on the brutal requirements of the Road Traffic Acts. Pettigrew, who had firmly announced that he was too old to attempt to learn, had watched his wife's struggles in a frame of mind in which hope for her success and fear for his own safety were neatly balanced. Meanwhile, the summer passed. The holiday had been planned for the end of June; by the time Eleanor was at last made free of the road August was over.

Even there, Pettigrew reflected, her luck had held. Summer had miraculously prolonged itself into September, for one thing. That, of course, was a phenomenon from which a good many other people had benefited. One could not suppose that it had been arranged peculiarly in Eleanor's favour. But it had surely been by some special dispensation of Providence that almost at a moment's notice she had been able to find rooms to let in a farmhouse on the very edge of Exmoor at the height of the stag-hunting season. He had tried to indicate to her how extraordinarily lucky she had been, but Eleanor, who disapproved of blood-sports and had yet to learn of their importance in the

economics of Exmoor, took her good fortune very much
for granted. That being so, Pettigrew, who tended to
become more secretive with advancing years, had not
thought it worth while to enlarge on the coincidence
that had brought him back to Sallowcombe after an
interval so long that it fairly terrified him to contemplate it. That period of his life, in any case, was so
remote that it had ceased to have any significance.
Everything had changed since then, himself most of all.
He came to the place as a complete newcomer. It was
better so.

None the less, it had been somewhat of a shock when
the car drew up before an entrance that seemed to have
shrunk in size with the years but in no other respect had
altered in the least. He had not thought that his recollection would be so clear. The shock had been even
greater when on penetrating inside he found everything
altered out of recognition. But it was a shock for the
most part of relief. As a realist he could only be thankful for the change. He had loved the place dearly in
those days, but he did not think that at his present age
he could have endured its rigours, and he was quite
certain that his wife could not. With a memory stimulated by his surroundings he recalled the Sallowcombe
of his youth, with its persistent smell of the stable, the
candles flickering in the fierce draughts, the lumpy
feather beds, each with its appropriate furniture beneath. He had thought it pure heaven then, but now . . .
Thank goodness for a comfortable mattress, he reflected,
as he wearily turned over for the tenth time, even if I
can't sleep on it.

Journey into the Past

But if the Sallowcombe of today, with its indoor sanitation, smart threepiece suites and the television set in the visitors' lounge, was a change from the ramshackle establishment of the past, the difference was as nothing beside the difference between its inhabitants of then and now. Pettigrew remembered of old a coarse, jovial, occasionally drunken couple, slightly larger than life, as the figures of one's childhood are apt to be, who had alternately fascinated and terrified him. Their geniality had been overwhelming, their rages alarming, and their vocabulary, particularly when in their cups, had contributed freely to his education. In the place of this Dickensian pair now reigned a sober, widowed butcher whose home was admirably administered for him and for his visitors by his sober, widowed daughter. They were dull in comparison, but it made for comfort.

Thinking it over as he lay there, Pettigrew, an inveterate analyser of his fellows, wondered whether they were quite so dull as at first appeared. Of Mr. Joliffe he had so far seen little, though he liked what he had seen. He was a serious, elderly man, with the pink fleshiness that master butchers always seem to acquire in the way of their profession; and he showed clearly by his speech that he was not a native of Exmoor but had come to it from somewhere "up country". (Or should the phrase be "down country"? Pettigrew, who had not heard it used for half a century, puzzled his sleepy brain with the problem for some time before deciding that it did not matter and that in any case the expression, as a local usage, was probably long out of date.) He was the owner of a good business in Whitsea, on the coast a dozen miles away, and his farm was auxiliary to the business, just as the letting of rooms to visitors was auxiliary to the farm. It had surprised Pettigrew a little that so obviously prosperous a man as Joliffe should have concerned himself with yet a third, and comparatively trivial source of income. But that evening he had accidentally witnessed a scene which revealed Joliffe as a person unlikely to overlook any financial question, large or small. One of his small granddaughters had left the electric light on in an empty room. The result had been an explosion of temper quite out of proportion to the offence. Clearly, there were some things that could disturb the massive calm with which Mr. Joliffe confronted the world, and those were things that touched his pocket.

The granddaughter had accepted the reproof very calmly. Evidently, at twelve, she had learned to be philosophical in such matters. If anybody had been upset, it was her mother. Quiet, shy, soft-spoken Mrs. Gorman was obviously completely devoted to her two young daughters. She was no less obviously in some dread of her masterful father. But quiet and submissive as she was, Pettigrew had little doubt that if it came to the point, she would be prepared to dare anything or anyone in her children's interests. She was, he judged, of the possessive type of mother, whose affection for her young would leave no room for any real interest in any other human being.

Having arrived at this satisfactory conclusion, Pettigrew must have dozed off, for when he opened his eyes

13

again the moonlight had vanished and in its place the first grey hint of dawn shewed through the window. It was very still and quiet. Only Eleanor's light breathing in the bed beside his own broke the silence. Yet he felt certain that he had been awakened by some noise, though he could not tell what. He lay listening for a moment or two and then his ear caught a small, grating sound from outside. In that instant, to his great surprise, he knew exactly what had made the sound and whence it came.

The back door of the farmhouse gave on to the farm-yard, and next to the back door was a tool shed with a gently sloping lead roof. The window of one of the bed-rooms in the older part of the house was immediately above that roof. For an active boy occupying the room who wanted to get in or out without his elders' know-ledge, or for whom the stairs were too dull and mundane a means of access, the tool shed made a convenient landing stage between ground and window. The recol-lection emerged sharp and keen from the depths of the past, provoked by the long-forgotten sound. Some-body was on the roof of the tool shed at that moment; and the room in question was not now occupied by a boy.

Pettigrew slipped out of bed without disturbing his wife, and peered out of window. The other side of the farmyard was in shadow, but he could just make out the line of the tool shed, and on the roof, pressed against the wall, the figure of a man. His head was level with the window, which was open at the bottom. He stood there motionless for a moment, and then in the semi-darkness

14

the upper part of his body seemed to blend with another shape that appeared at the window. Pettigrew could just distinguish the pallor of two white arms that enfolded his head and shoulders. An instant later they were withdrawn, the window closed silently, the man dropped to the ground and vanished into the shadows.

"Good morning, sir! Good morning, madam! It's a lovely day and I've brought you your tea. Have you slept well? Would you be wanting eggs for breakfast or there's a nice piece of liver and bacon if you'd fancy that?"

Mrs. Gorman cooed as gently as a sucking dove. Pettigrew sat up in bed and contemplated that demure, slightly melancholy face, the calm, unruffled brow, the infinitely respectable demeanour. Anybody less like the heroine of an illicit love affair it would be hard to imagine. But he knew the layout of the house too well to have any doubt as to which was Mrs. Gorman's room. His judgment of character had been hopelessly at fault—not for the first time, he conceded. He felt at once irritated and amused. It was like living in a short story by Somerset Maugham.

As he dressed, his mind turned to the problem of the man's identity. In a remote spot such as this there could not be many candidates. . . .

"How many people does Mr. Joliffe employ on the farm, do you suppose?" he said to Eleanor at breakfast.

"Two or three, I think," she said. "There's an old

15

man who milks the cows and a girl who drives the tractor."

"Isn't there a young, able-bodied man on the farm?"

"I don't know. Why do you ask?"

"I was just wondering," said Pettigrew.

CHAPTER II

The Hunt is Up

Mrs. Gorman was right. It was a lovely day, and on such a day a picnic lunch was clearly indicated. When Eleanor went into the kitchen to suggest it to Mrs. Gorman she found that Doreen, the twelve year old, was already preparing the basket.

"The meet's at Satcherley Way, so you'll want to leave by half-past ten," she explained.

"The meet?" said Eleanor, puzzled.

"The *meet*," Doreen repeated, her large eyes round with surprise at such stupidity. "The meet of the stag-hounds. Didn't you see the card in the hall?"

"But what makes you think we want to go to the meet, Doreen?"

"Visitors always do."

"Well this one doesn't. I don't like hunting, and neither does Mr. Pettigrew."

"Cor!" said Doreen, in a tone of incredulity.

So that there should be no doubt about the matter, Eleanor took the precaution of finding Satcherley Way on the map before they set out, and the picnic took place at a spot which seemed reasonably remote from the contaminated area. So far as her husband was

concerned, it was an immense success. The food was
good, the weather was warm, the heather on which
they reclined was deliciously soft and yielding. Decidedly the holiday had been an excellent idea of
Eleanor's. If only he had been able to sleep better the
night before. . . .

"Wake up, Frank," said Eleanor a little later.

"My dear, I am wide awake. I have never been anything else."

"Then you should not have been snoring. What was
that noise I heard just now?"

"Obviously, I should have thought, my snoring. Or
do you mean something else?"

"I do mean something else. Listen!"

Pettigrew was well awake by now, and straining his
ears. In a moment he heard the sound, distant but clear
and quite unmistakable.

"That was the horn," he said.

"A horn, did you say?"

"Yes." Actually, Pettigrew realized, he had said, not
"a horn", but "*the* horn". It came to him with a little
hock of recollection that there was a world of difference
between the two. "A hunting horn. Perhaps they're
running this way."

"I hope not," said Eleanor chillingly. "It must be a
disgusting sight. But they may not be chasing a stag at
all. The man was probably only blowing to call the
dogs together."

"No." Pettigrew was quite decided on the point.
"Hounds are running all right. He was doubling his
horn." (The phrase slipped easily off his tongue—

18

fantastically easy for one who had not used it for fifty years.)

"Frank!"

"Yes, my love?" Pettigrew turned from looking at the distant ridge of moorland to see his wife's brilliant blue eyes fixed on him accusingly.

"You seem to know a lot about this stag-hunting business. Have you been deceiving me all this time?"

"God forbid!"

"Have you ever been a huntsman?"

"Heavens, no! A huntsman is a highly skilled professional. I've only had one profession all my life. You know that."

"Don't quibble, Frank. You know what I mean. Have you ever been a hunter?"

"No, of course not! A hunter is—— All right, I won't quibble. I do know what you mean. I will be honest. I have hunted. And with these hounds, too. But it was a long time ago."

"How long?"

"Longer than I care to think. When that I was a little tiny boy. My father used to bring us down here for the holidays."

"And you hunted," said Eleanor reproachfully.

"If you can call it hunting. I was put on a pony and bumped about the moor after the hounds. One hadn't much choice in the matter. Everybody did it."

"I see." Eleanor sounded mollified by his explanation. "You don't sound as if you enjoyed it very much."

"I wouldn't say that," said Pettigrew slowly. . . .

How fantastic to suppose that he had forgotten all

about it! With the scent of the heather in his nostrils, the sound of the horn fresh in his ears, gazing across the valley at two distant hummocks which suddenly revealed themselves as the very oldest of old acquaintances, Pettigrew found his memory opening up like some monstrous flower, fold within fold. He saw himself, a small boy, jogging uncomfortably to the meet along a road innocent of motor traffic but thick with dust on a hard-mouthed, self-willed pony that could not accommodate its pace to that of the big hunter alongside. It was a pony given to habits so unpleasing and undignified that even in retrospect he averted his mind from them; but once away, it would gallop for ever. The boy was wearing what struck him now as fantastically uncomfortable clothes—a hard hat that seared his forehead, breeches that pinched his flesh below the knees, gaiters that never quite spanned the gap between the breeches and the heavy black boots. In his leather gloves he clutched a thonged hunting crop that was at once his greatest pride and an appalling encumbrance. One pocket was weighed down with a vast pocket knife equipped among other things with a hook designed to take stones out of horses' hooves; another bulged tightly over the packet of sandwiches, which, when eaten later in the day, would prove, whatever their composition, to taste of leather gloves and smell of sweating pony. His secret hope was that someone would give him for his birthday a man's-size sandwich box in a leather container which could be strapped to the saddle. The ultimate glory of a hunting flask might be attained next season, perhaps.

20

The Hunt is Up

Pettigrew could see the boy in his mind's eye with remarkable clarity, except for one particular—his face. But if the features altogether escaped him, he could be sure of the expression, which he knew to be one of intense solemnity, the expression of the participant in a sacred rite. Had he enjoyed it? That was the very question they used to ask him at the end of the day, he remembered. He had always said "Yes", as a matter of course, before stripping off those agonizing breeches and plunging into a hot mustard bath. It was the answer they expected. But even then he had known how hopelessly inadequate the word "enjoy" was. One "enjoyed" so many things—parties, theatres, the common pleasures of life. Hunting was a thing apart—a compound of excitement and terror, discomfort and ecstasy, boredom and bliss. . . .

"Well?" said Eleanor.

By now the picture of the small boy was becoming overlaid in Pettigrew's mind with a host of other images—his father's old-fashioned, full-skirted hunting coat, the Henry Alken prints in the Sallowcombe dining-room, the echo of the peculiar wail of the Vicar's voice at Mattins. With an effort he came back to the present and looked for inspiration across the valley towards Tucker's Barrows. (How could he have forgotten that household name for an instant? he asked himself.) But the view gave him no help in self-expression. Rather flatly he said at last:

"Actually, it was rather fun."

"Fun!"

There was something in his wife's voice that made

21

Pettigrew add hastily, "Fun for a boy of that age, of course, I mean."

"But even at that age, Frank, did you not realize the pointlessness, the wanton cruelty of the whole thing?"

"No, I certainly didn't. Boys don't, you know, unless there is someone about to point it out to them."

"I suppose not. Girls are different, of course."

Pettigrew, remembering certain female cousins among whom he had been brought up, opened his mouth to speak and then thought better of it.

In the silence that fell between them he became aware of a variety of small sounds—the buzzing of an intrusive fly, the plash of water from the stream in the combe below, and finally the sound for which, without realizing it, he had been straining his ears for minutes past—the faint whimper of hounds. It came for a moment only and was not repeated. Pettigrew was not surprised. Wherever they were running, he reflected, it was an even chance that it was uphill and through long heather or bracken. They would have little breath to spare to give tongue on a warm afternoon like this. It was, of course, a matter of complete indifference to him whether they were running, or in what direction; but he found himself none the less concentrating his attention upon a particular part of the skyline where the ground dipped to form a saddle between the Barrows and another, less prominent eminence. The latter point he recognized at once, in his mood of reawakened sensitivity to the past. It was called Bolter's Tussock; and astonishingly enough, the absurd name evoked a thoroughly disagreeable sensation in his mind. Alone in that wide prospect of familiar, friendly scenes the place stood for something vaguely but unquestionably sinister. Something had occurred there so unpleasant that he had long since buried the recollection of it deep in his subconscious mind. Painfully and perversely he struggled to disinter it. He was almost on the point of success when the present intruded upon the past, and temporarily blotted it out. An object appeared momentarily on the skyline at the very point that he had selected for attention, and began to move at a steep angle down the slope opposite to where they sat. Pettigrew leapt to his feet, startling Eleanor, who had begun to assemble the contents of the picnic basket.

"There he goes!" he exclaimed.

Eleanor looked up, and after some little difficulty Pettigrew succeeded in pointing out the deer to her just before it disappeared in the wood of stunted oaks that clothed the lower slopes of the valley.

"Oh, the poor thing!" she said softly.

Pettigrew said nothing. Already the leading hounds were racing down the slope from the brow of the hill, not half a minute behind their quarry. Barring a miracle, the stag was doomed, though there might yet be an hour's tow-row down the water before he was booked. It was no use being sentimental about it. But telling himself so did not prevent him feeling sentimental, all the same. It was all of fifty years since he had last seen a hunted deer and now the sight of it had in some way dispelled the enchantment of reminiscence in which he had been living up to that moment. Willy-nilly, he found himself looking at the hapless beast

23

through the eyes of the elderly, urban humanitarian who had somehow evolved from that small boy. He had forgotten that a stag looked so defenceless, lumbering along with its curious stiff-legged canter in front of the pitiless pack. A shrill squeal from below announced that someone had viewed the deer on his way down the valley, and he felt a sudden stab of pity for the victim.

This is quite illogical, he told himself. I shouldn't feel a bit like this for a hare, and if it was a fox I should have probably screamed my head off by now. Why the distinction? He pondered the problem gravely, while the field streamed across the slope opposite and clattered down the track that led through the wood. On serious reflection, he came to the conclusion that it was a question of size. A deer was altogether too big to hunt with a clear conscience. In sport one should always kill something a good deal smaller than oneself, something that succumbed easily, quickly, anonymously. A stag was too large to be anything but an individual, his death too difficult to be other than a prolonged personal affair.

"Honestly now, Frank," said Eleanor, "what do you think of it?"

"I think," said her husband deliberately, "that it would be much worse if they were elephants."

It was quite impossible to tell from Eleanor's expression what, if anything, she made of this remark. By way of reply, she picked up the rug on which they had been sitting, shook it free of crumbs and returned it to the car.

"The last of the hunters has gone," she said. "I think

we've seen all that there is to see. Shall we be getting
back?"

"By all means."

"You're sure you want to? You don't want to—to
walk it off before you come home?"

"Walk it off? What do you mean?"

"Come, Frank, you know perfectly well."

Pettigrew looked at his wife in silence for a moment.
Then he acknowledged defeat with a shrug of his
shoulders.

"To be honest, I do," he said. "What beats me is how
you know."

"It's pretty obvious, isn't it? You're suffering from a
bad attack of—I suppose the psychologists have in-
vented a technical term for it, but I should call it
nostalgia. You've been living in a dream world of
your own ever since we arrived at Sallowcombe. Was
that where you used to stay when you were small, by
the way?"

"You know perfectly well that it was," said Pettigrew,
a shade bitterly. "I thought that I was being decently
reticent about it, and all the time it appears that I've
been making life quite intolerable for you by my senti-
mentalizing. I apologize."

"Don't be absurd, Frank, there is nothing to apologize for. Only it struck me, especially since this stag-
hunting business began, that perhaps there was a ghost
that wanted laying and you might be happier if you
went ghost-hunting by yourself."

Francis Pettigrew was staring across the valley again
in the direction from which the stag had appeared.

"A ghost!" he reflected. "Do you know, Eleanor, you are a great deal nearer the truth than even you have any business to be. There *is* a ghost, and I've only just remembered what it is."

He picked up the picnic basket and, walking over to the car, got into the passenger seat. Eleanor took her place at the wheel.

"So you've decided not to walk?" she said.

"I intend to walk," he replied, "but not from here. We'll drive round the head of the combe, and you can put me down near Bolter's Tussock."

"But that's taking you away from Sallowcombe."

"Not as much as you'd think. There's quite a good cross-country track past Tucker's Barrows that cuts off a mile of road. I shall manage it very well."

Eleanor started the car and they set off. Presently she asked: "Is there any particular virtue in Bolter's Tussock that makes you want to start your walk there?"

"I don't know that you'd call it a virtue, exactly, but it has one excellent qualification for ghost-laying."

"What is that?"

"Obviously, that it should be haunted."

They drove some distance in silence before Pettigrew spoke again.

"As you have not asked what I mean, I assume that you intend to rely on your usual uncanny methods to find out. I propose in this case to thwart you by the simple expedient of telling you outright. The plain fact is that I was more horribly frightened at Bolter's Tussock than I have ever been in my life."

"What by? Did your pony run away with you?"

The Hunt is Up

"Actually, the pony did bolt—and anyone who thinks *that* isn't a frightening experience has no imagination. But that was afterwards. The real horror came first."

"Don't tell me about it if you'd rather not."

"Good Lord, I've no objection to talking about it now! The interesting thing is that this is literally the first time I have ever mentioned it to anybody. I was much too scared at the time to say anything, and after that I must have bottled it up inside me so successfully that I ended by forgetting it altogether—until about ten minutes ago. Memory's a funny thing, isn't it? Perhaps that suppressed memory was at the back of the hideous nightmares that used to plague me at school."

"Perhaps," said Eleanor a trifle acidly. "But I shouldn't like to give an opinion till you'd told me what 'it' was."

" 'It' was simply a dead man."

"On Bolter's Tussock?"

"Yes."

"What was it doing there?"

"I have no idea—I never found out."

"And you—you just left it there?"

"I left very quickly, when the pony bolted."

"But somebody else must have found it, even if you said nothing. Didn't you read about it in the papers or hear people talking about it?"

"One doesn't read the papers much at that age, except the cricket scores, and I didn't listen to what my elders said about things like that."

"You seem to have been remarkably incurious."

27

The Hunt is Up

"Incurious! Good God, woman, can't you understand? I was terrified. I didn't want to know any more about it. I was convinced that if anything came out, I should be made in some way responsible. For days afterwards I couldn't see a policeman without being certain that he was going to ask me about the body on Bolter's Tussock. Every time my father opened a newspaper I was sure he would read out an account of it, and turn on me with some deadly question which would end in my being hauled off to prison. And then time went by—it can't have been more than a week or so, really, but it seemed longer—and the holidays were over, and I was safe back at prep school and nothing had happened."

He stopped abruptly and looked out of the window.

"All right, you can put me down here," he said.

He got out of the car. In the bright autumn sun, Bolter's Tussock, above and to the left of where he stood, looked as innocent and peaceful as any strip of moorland could well do. From far down the valley a distant cry of hounds told him that the hunt was still afoot.

"Have a good walk," said Eleanor. "And don't be too disappointed if——"

"If what?"

"If there's nothing there after all."

CHAPTER III

Minster Tracy

Having left her husband to walk home, Eleanor took the opportunity to carry out a plan which had long been in her mind. She would call on Hester Greenway.

Hester Greenway had been Eleanor's best friend at school. She had not seen her for a long time, but they had kept in touch over the years. They remembered each other's birthdays, and every Christmas brought from Hester not only a small hand-made gift in impeccable taste but a long, chatty letter. Frank had never met her, and it is regrettably to be recorded that he had taken a strong dislike to her, solely on the strength of her taste in Christmas presents and her epistolary style. For this reason, Eleanor had seen fit to say nothing to him of the arrangement by which she was now driving, not back to Sallowcombe, but to Minster Tracy.

Following the directions she had been given, Eleanor turned off the main road down a lane that led her into a deep valley. As she rounded a bend, she saw below her Tracy Church, embowered in trees, the inevitable stream purling past its west door. Hester's father had been vicar of the parish, which after his death had been amalgamated with another, because its small and dwindling population could not support an incumbent

29

of its own. Eleanor knew all this, and that Minster Tracy was reputed to be the second smallest church in England; but she had not expected anything quite so tiny or so lonely. The minute church was surrounded by a well-filled churchyard, but she could see no living habitation. Only when she had almost reached it did she notice a pair of stone pillars marking the entrance to a drive that led to a house of some substance set well back from the road. A little further on, the furious barking of a Sealyham terrier announced her arrival at Hester's little house.

Eleanor had not been prepared for the Sealyham. Hester had not betrayed any interest in dogs during their schooldays, or in that never-to-be-forgotten fortnight in Florence which had been the highlight of their friendship. Herself not a dog-lover, she was perhaps unreasonably surprised to find that Hester had become one. She found that it was not the only respect in which her friend had changed. It was natural enough that she should have become countrified, and in the process have somewhat aged, but need her form be quite so tweedy, her face so weatherbeaten?

Oddly enough, Miss Greenway, though hospitable enough in her welcome, seemed to find cause for comment in the changes which the years had wrought in Eleanor.

"Good old Ellie!" she cried as she came to the door. "My word, but anyone can see with half an eye that you're married! Let's see, how long is it now? Ten years? Twelve? Who would have thought it? Down, Jeannie, down!" she went on to the Sealyham. "Go to your basket! Isn't she a ripping little bitch? Three litters I've had from her, and do the pups sell! You've never embarked on a family, have you, Ellie? I dare say you're right, but it seems rather a shame to have got the matronly figure with nothing to shew for it."

Eleanor, who had not been called Ellie since she was in Upper Fifth, said in non-committal tones that she was very well and that Hester also looked well.

"I'm blooming, thanks. So I should be with all the fresh air and exercise I get. You'd be all the better for it, Ellie, and thinner, I shouldn't wonder. Where's your husband? Out with the hounds, I suppose?"

"No, Frank doesn't hunt."

"Doesn't he? Why not?"

Eleanor drew breath to explain her views on hunting, but Hester gave her no opportunity to express them.

"I suppose he's like me and can't afford to," she said. "I get the loan of a pony at the fag-end of the season sometimes, and what's the good of that?"

Eleanor gave it up. Her old friend was hopelessly coarsened and depraved. She began to wish that she had not come. And then, quite unexpectedly, things took a turn for the better. Hester began to talk about the past, and soon convinced her that she had not lost all regard for the finer things of life. She remembered Florence with enthusiasm and accuracy, had been buying some quite expensive reproductions of Renaissance masters, and shamed Eleanor altogether by proving that she had kept up the study of Italian which she, Eleanor, had long neglected. And her interest in the fine arts was not confined to Italy.

31

"Come and have a look at the church," she commanded. "There's a very decent thirteenth-century font, and what I say is a leper's squint, though the experts won't admit it."

Miss Greenway proved an excellent guide to the church, though Eleanor could well have dispensed with the anecdote about a vixen in the pulpit which she insisted on telling. But the second smallest church in England does not take very long to explore, and they were soon out in the sun again. As they walked through the churchyard Eleanor's eye was caught by an imposingly ugly polished granite tombstone. It bore the name of Ephraim Gorman. Just beyond it, and scarcely less expensive, was the memorial stone of Samuel Gorman. A broken marble pillar, evidently of slightly earlier date, proved to mark the grave of Job Gorman and his wife Sarah.

"They all seem to be Gormans here," she remarked. "They must be a very large family."

"Very large and very quarrelsome," Hester replied. "They intermarry all over the place, and go to law with one another at the drop of a hat. They all come back here to be buried, though. My father always used to say that a Gorman funeral was the most typical family gathering. The only completely comfortable member of the party was the deceased, because like all the others he wasn't on speaking terms with anybody else, but he didn't have to pretend that he was. Which reminds me, there'll be another Gorman funeral here before long."

"Has one of them died?"

"Not yet, so far as I know, but he can't hold out much longer. Gilbert, my landlord, is about on his last legs, the doctor tells me. He lives at the Manor, the house you saw as you came down the hill. No children, so goodness knows who gets the place when he goes—I shouldn't wonder if it meant another lawsuit."

"Then the Mrs. Gorman at Sallowcombe, Mr. Joliffe's daughter, married into this family? I suppose her husband is buried somewhere here?"

"What, Jack Gorman? Good Lord, no! He's very much alive and kicking—too much so for some people's tastes. He got a girl into trouble down at Brockenford only the other day. Oh, he's quite a lad, is Jack."

Hester's attitude of approval towards the backslidings of a husband and father shocked Eleanor profoundly. They were unworthy of her old school friend, altogether unsuitable for a parson's daughter. As they strolled back again to Hester's cottage, she shut her ears to yet another regrettably earthy anecdote and came to a firm conclusion. She would not stay to tea.

Hester took the decision with calm. Possibly she was as disappointed in Eleanor as Eleanor with her, but for different reasons. She bade her goodbye affectionately, expressed the hope that they would meet again soon and added some directions for an interesting variant on the route back to Sallowcombe.

There followed an anticlimax. The car refused to start.

"What a bore!" Hester observed, after watching

Eleanor's struggles in silence for some time. "It looks as if you'll have to stay to tea after all, Ellie. No good asking me to help. I don't know the first thing about cars."

"Where's the nearest garage?" asked Eleanor.

"Jock Blackadder's. It's only five miles away, but he's pretty sure to be out with the hounds. I'll ring him up and make sure, though."

She was away for a few minutes, during which Eleanor became more conscious than ever of the remoteness of Minster Tracy.

"No go," Hester reported. "I've just remembered something, though. The odd-job man at the Manor will be coming in about now to give the pigs their afternoon feed. He's a wizard with machinery. Let's toddle up there and ask him to come down."

Wearily Eleanor set off with her in search of the odd-job man, but they did not need to go so far. They were barely in sight of the Manor gateposts when a green tradesman's van swung out of the drive, turned in their direction and stopped in response to their wavings. A familiar face looked down from the driver's seat.

"Mr. Joliffe!" Eleanor exclaimed. "This is a bit of luck!"

Mr. Joliffe' expression was usually serious. On this occasion it was positively melancholy.

"If you say so, Mrs. Pettigrew," he remarked. "It's certainly a chance my being here to-day. It's not often I come this way."

"Mrs. Pettigrew has broken down outside my front door," Hester explained.

34

"I can't give her a lift home, I'm afraid," said Mr. Joliffe. "I've got to get back to the shop before closing time. Saturday is a busy time for us. But I'll see if I can do anything to put the trouble right. I'll give you a lift down."

There was barely room for three in the front of the van, but they contrived to squeeze themselves in. Hester merrily proposed that she should sit in the back among the joints of meat, but Mr. Joliffe was conspicuously not amused at the suggestion.

"Have you been visiting the sick at the Manor?" Hester asked. "How did you find Gilbert?"

"Poorly," said Mr. Joliffe with mournful satisfaction. "He's not long for this world."

"Jolly good of you to come all this way, with petrol the price it is," Hester went on. She pinched Eleanor as she spoke, so that there could be no doubt that a joke was intended.

"Obviously it wouldn't have been worth the petrol to make a special journey just to see how Gilbert Gorman was," said Mr. Joliffe seriously. "But it so happened that the Staghunters Hotel rang up this afternoon to say they had three coach parties come in unexpected and would be out of meat for the weekend if I couldn't give them a special delivery. I thought I might as well come this way and look in on the Grange while I was about it."

"And do some courting of Louisa at the same time," Hester suggested.

Eleanor felt acutely uncomfortable. Hester's bucolic humour was even more painful than the pinches that

35

punctuated it. But Mr. Joliffe seemed to have a skin that was quite impervious to her blunted shafts. He did not so much as change colour. Fortunately, before any further witticisms could be uttered, they had reached the car and to this Mr. Joliffe now turned his grave attention. In rather less than five minutes he diagnosed and cured the trouble, while the helpless females looked on in uncomprehending admiration.

"A choked jet," he explained, wiping his pink, plump fingers on a piece of cotton waste. "You won't have any more trouble."

Eleanor was profuse in her thanks. "You are a genius, Mr. Joliffe," she said.

Mr. Joliffe was as insensible to flattery as to raillery. "Just a hard-working man," he said. "I reckon to save twenty pounds a year by doing my own running repairs. Good day, Miss Greenway. I shall see you this evening, I hope, Mrs. Pettigrew."

He drove off, and the atmosphere felt lighter for the removal of his solid, overpowering presence. Jeannie, who had removed herself to the back premises at his approach, celebrated his departure by rushing out with a paroxysm of barking.

"That man always brings out the worst in me," Hester observed. "He's so *worthy*. I wish he would marry Louisa Gorman, though. She's about the one woman I know who could keep him under. Goodbye, Ellie. Come again soon."

Eleanor's homeward route took her across Bolter's Tussock. The westering sun was in her eyes as she

36

came out on to the open moor at the top of the slope. Thus it was that only at the last moment did she put on her brakes in time to avoid a pale-faced mud-splashed man who tottered out into the road in front of her.

"Frank, darling!" she exclaimed. "What have you been up to now?"

CHAPTER IV

The Find

Pettigrew watched the car out of sight round a bend in the road, and then set himself to climb the short but steep slope in front of him. He was walking here on thin, wiry grass, made slippery by a month's drought, and it was more of an effort than he had bargained for. He told himself very firmly that it was delightful to be walking again on Exmoor. He repeated it—rather defiantly—when one foot sank ankle deep in a boggy patch that mysteriously maintained itself on an otherwise arid hillside. After stopping to admire the view for the third time, he qualified it by the admission that for a man of his age Bolter's Tussock was a good deal too far from the nearest road for comfort.

Then, as he gazed up towards the heathery plateau which seemed scarcely nearer than when he had started, something appeared momentarily on the skyline and was gone again with a gleam of sun on glass. It was so unexpected that it took him an appreciable time to recognize it. But there could be no doubt. It was a motor car, or rather the upper half of one, travelling on a road which must be lying just beyond the crest of the hill, a place where no road should have been—or at least where none had been when Pettigrew was last there. To prove that it was no optical illusion, two packed coaches followed in its wake a moment later.

His first reaction to the discovery that Bolter's Tussock was in fact now about the most easily accessible spot on the moor was one of blind, irrational rage. A road! A highway across Bolter's Tussock! The thing seemed a sheer indecency. Was nothing sacred nowadays? He stood there, fuming impotently, while several more vehicles crossed and recrossed the once hallowed spot, until the absurdity of the situation struck him, and he laughed aloud.

This was what happened, he told himself, when an elderly crock revisited the scenes of his childhood, and was naïve enough to think that he could revive, unchanged, the emotions that the child had experienced. First he discovered that his legs and lungs were barely equal to what had once been an easy walk; then that a very sensible piece of road engineering had made the walk unnecessary. He was a fool to have expected anything else, and a sentimentalist to regret it. All the same, if changes there had to be, he wished that they could have come anywhere else than to Bolter's Tussock. As a boy, even before it had become associated with the first genuine fear that he had known, the place had had for him a quality of loneliness and mystery. He remembered how he had prided himself on the fact—real or fancied—that the name was a purely local usage and did not appear on the maps, so that only the truly initiate could even utter it. Now it was probably scheduled as a fare stage for buses. It was ridiculous to be upset by such a thing, but he felt upset, none the less. Rather melodramatically, he allowed himself the luxury of a deep sigh.

The sigh was echoed loudly from somewhere close at hand. He looked round in surprise but saw nothing to account for it. The noise was repeated, and followed this time by a throaty gurgle that, like so many things he had seen and heard that day, seemed to belong to the past. Then over the curve of the hillside above him appeared a face—an innocent, enquiring face, topped with a dark forelock that tumbled over a narrow forehead between two mild brown eyes—a long narrow face, terminating in the light-tan muzzle that is traditionally held to mark the Exmoor pony.

Pettigrew stared at the newcomer, who stared back at him, and then began haltingly to advance in his direction. At first glance it seemed remarkably like the pony whose odd characteristics he had been recalling shortly before, but he realized almost at once that it must be larger, several—what did they call them?—*hands* larger, in fact, unless he, Pettigrew, had mysteriously shrunk to the size of the small boy who had once ridden that pony. In other respects, the illusion was singularly complete. Like its predecessor, this was a half-bred Exmoor pony—always supposing that such a thing as a pure-bred Exmoor existed, as to which he seemed to recollect some controversy. This animal had thrown its rider, just as the other had been wont to do. It was stumbling because one fore leg was caught up in the trailing reins—a phenomenon which

The Find

Pettigrew had had occasion to observe before. And as he had done more than once in those distant days, Pettigrew was now advancing upon it, uttering deprecating sounds.

The pony displayed no reluctance to be caught, thereby showing another marked distinction from the one that bulked so large in Pettigrew's memory. Not only that, but it actually consented to stand stock still while he clumsily lifted one fore leg and released it from the reins. Either the breed had become noticeably milder with the years, he reflected, or this particular specimen must be too exhausted to resent handling. He slipped the reins over its head and examined his capture. To judge from its condition, it had been down in a bog recently, but it showed no signs of distress, although it was sweating freely. He patted its neck, and the beast responded by nearly knocking him over with a gesture of its head that was apparently intended to be friendly. He found an apple left over from lunch in his pocket, and their relations became positively affectionate.

"Well, Dobbin, and what do I do with you now?" Pettigrew asked.

The only reply that Dobbin could think of, apparently, was to thrust his nose in the direction of the now empty pocket and sneeze damply over Pettigrew's coat. It was well-intentioned, but not particularly helpful.

He looked about him. The moor, which so recently had been alive with horsemen, horsewomen and not a few horsechildren, was now to all appearances deserted. There seemed little point now in going back to the road as he had intended. Even if after this delay he got there in time to cut off Eleanor, he could hardly abandon Dobbin to his fate. The better course, and the kinder one, seemed to be to press on up the hill in the hope of finding his late rider. Looking at the saddle and bridle and still judging this pony by the one that he remembered best, he came to the conclusion that they must have parted company fairly recently. Had it been otherwise, he reasoned, Dobbin would by now have shed a stirrup leather rolling in a bog-hole, if not burst his girth and got rid of the saddle altogether. At the very least, he would have trodden on the reins sufficiently hard and often to snap them. Yet the harness was in perfect order, though as worn and ancient as the equipment of hireling animals is apt to be. Warm with the conscious rectitude of a good Samaritan, Pettigrew took Dobbin by the bridle, turned him round and began to walk him back in the direction from which he had appeared.

The pony came willingly enough—from Pettigrew's point of view a thought too willingly. It was the old difficulty of trying to accommodate the paces of two animals of very different natural gaits, and, willing as he might be, accommodation was not Dobbin's strong point. He walked uphill about twice as fast as Pettigrew was prepared to go, and when checked threw his head about in a most uncomfortable and alarming fashion. Moreover, he had a disconcerting habit of monopolizing the only semblance of a track that there was and pushing his escort off it with a broad, hard and very smelly shoulder. The walk soon showed every sign of degenerating into a thoroughly undignified contest, in which Pettigrew got the worst of every round.

He pulled angrily at the bridle and Dobbin consented to stop. After giving Pettigrew a glance which might be interpreted as pitying or contemptuous according to fancy, he put his head down and began to munch contentedly at the very unattractive-looking herbage. Pettigrew formed a desperate resolution. There was, after all, only one suitable method of getting about on Exmoor, and, aged as he was, he proposed to employ it—at least, as far as the top of the hill. He gathered up the end of the reins in his hand, contrived to get his toe into the stirrup iron and laboriously heaved himself on to the pony's back.

Dobbin's reaction to this performance was reassuringly placid. He continued with his meal as though nothing had happened, until Pettigrew drew his attention to the change in affairs by hauling on the reins. He then consented to raise his head and, stimulated by a kick in the ribs, began to walk sedately up the hill.

For the next few minutes Pettigrew was fully occupied in keeping the pony's head in the right direction. Dobbin now began to display a tendency to veer away down the slope, and when thwarted in this objective was apt to stop and resume his interrupted grazing. Pettigrew recognized with regret that his control of his steed was not all that it might have been. He was unprovided with a stick. His legs, the means by which, he seemed to remember, the true horseman could always convey his intentions to his mount, seemed quite inadequate to their task—possibly because the stirrup leathers were too short. As to the reins, he felt that they would have been more effective if the bit to which they were connected had not been a plain snaffle bar and Dobbin's mouth not been so uncompromisingly hard. None the less, by cajolery, diplomacy and persistence, he contrived to achieve his purpose. Gradually the slope grew easier, the grass gave way to bracken, the bracken to ling, and he had arrived.

Pettigrew pulled Dobbin to a standstill and looked around him with deep satisfaction. This was the Exmoor of half a century ago—unchanged, unspoilt. By some trick of the landscape, even the offending road had disappeared behind a fold in the ground, and only an occasional murmur betrayed the passing of traffic from time to time. For the rest, there was—not silence, but a background of sounds appropriate to the scene—the constant murmur of water from below, the mew of a buzzard floating high overhead, and, once again, and not so very far away, the horn.

The pony evidently heard the horn, too, for he threw his head in the air and showed a disposition to move on. Pettigrew restrained him, and took the opportunity to lengthen his leathers by a couple of holes. With his legs in a normal position, he began to feel at ease in the saddle—astonishingly so, considering how long it was since he had last crossed a horse's back. Riding, like swimming, was presumably one of the things that one did not forget, even after the passage of years. The feeling of confidence was altogether delightful. He clicked his tongue, plucked at the bridle, and found himself moving forward at a smart trot.

It did just pass through Pettigrew's mind, as he set off, that somewhere on the moor there was wandering, dismounted and disconsolate, a man—or woman—to whom in due course he would have to surrender his mount. He even remembered that when that time came, the leathers would have to be shortened to their former length. But for the moment, there was nobody in sight, and almost at once he ceased altogether to give any thought to the hapless unknown whose misfortune had presented him with his ride. It might be said, indeed, that he ceased to have any rational thought at all, for from the moment that Dobbin began to step out he was in the full grip of the obsession that had been haunting him all day.

With one half of his mind he was perfectly well aware that he was an elderly, retired lawyer, quite unsuitably dressed for equestrian exercise—the silly pompous phrase floated before him, as plain as print—who was going to be extremely stiff next day if he continued to canter over rough ground in that fashion. (Exactly when the trot had turned into a canter he could not say. It must have been when he was thinking of something else.) With the other half, he was re-living intensely and vividly the experiences of half a century before. At intervals throughout the afternoon he had been doing no less; but now it was with a difference. For whereas then he had been eagerly snatching at every scrap of the past that memory brought back to his mind, consciously and pleasurably building up the

45

The Find

vanished scene, now he found the images of the past pouring in upon him unbidden—and unwelcome. Back once more on Bolter's Tussock, on horseback, he positively did not want to be reminded of what had happened the last time he had been there. The experience had been altogether too violent and too unpleasant. It came back to him now in extraordinary detail.

It wasn't a hunting day, he remembered, just an ordinary afternoon towards the end of the holidays. He had been out on some errand or another and was on his way home to Sallowcombe, taking a short cut across the Tussock, cantering casually along with loose rein and looser legs, thinking of nothing in particular. Certainly not thinking of where he was going—the pony knew that without being told—nor of how he was riding. And then, in a flash, it had happened. The pony's smooth gait had been violently broken as he propped out his fore legs and stopped, for all the world as though he were refusing at a jump, sliding forward the last foot or two with his neck extended outwards and downwards for what seemed an immense distance. And the boy on his back had slid too, down that end-less neck, almost to the ground. Somehow he had saved himself, somehow struggled back eventually into the saddle, but in recollection it seemed that he had hung suspended there for a long time, head downwards, his face within a foot or two of another face, blindly staring up at him from the heather. It was in this guise that Francis Pettigrew had encountered death for the first time.

The Find

It is usually inadvisable to think about one thing while doing another, unless the thing being done is so familiar that its performance is virtually automatic. Riding, to someone completely out of practice, is best treated as a full-time occupation. Pettigrew in a normal mood was perfectly familiar with these truisms, but his mood at this moment was anything but normal. The pony's violent shy took him completely by surprise. It was only by the narrowest margin that he saved himself from going over its head. As he strove to recover himself he saw out of the corner of his eye what it was that had frightened it. He had time for a glimpse only, but it was enough. As in a nightmare, he realized that once more there was a dead man on Bolter's Tussock. The next instant he was at grips with another emergency. History repeated itself remorselessly. The pony bolted.

CHAPTER V

A Check

Pettigrew was not seriously alarmed at first. He realized that the unpredictable creature between his legs was momentarily out of control, but it seemed impossible that a mere pony could so remain for long with the weight of a full-grown man on its back. He had only to keep his head—and his seat—and all would be well. He was soon undeceived. The pony's first few strides carried it up a slight rise and nearly on to the road, which suddenly appeared from nowhere almost under its feet. Then for some inexplicable reason, instead of continuing forwards, it swerved away suddenly to the left, and plunged onwards across the Tussock, over the brow of the hill and down the other side.

About half way down a slope that grew progressively steeper every instant, Pettigrew experienced real fear. He knew that he could not stop the pony. With a sudden qualm at the pit of his stomach he realized that the pony could now almost certainly not stop itself. At this speed and on this declivity, a fall was inevitable. Leaning back in his saddle, hauling till his arms ached at the iron-mouthed brute, he had a sudden, swift recollection of a drawing by Leech, depicting just such a scene as he must present—an incompetent rider

48

being run away with down a steep incline. He could even remember the wording of the legend beneath: *Our friend Mr. Noddy has a day with the Brookside Harriers. With his usual prudence he gets a horse accustomed to the hills.* The vision of Mr. Noddy vanished in a spasm of sheer terror as he felt his mount's hind legs sink beneath him. They slid for a yard or two down the hillside, in a miniature avalanche of earth and stones, and then the pony seemed to crumple up altogether as the descent ended abruptly on a piece of hard and level ground.

In some extraordinary fashion Pettigrew had contrived to stay in the saddle up to the end, and in the saddle he remained while the pony scrambled back on to its feet. It was an open question which of the two was in the worse shape. Pettigrew was barely able to sit upright. His heart was thumping in the most alarming manner, and there was a strange roaring sound in his ears. The pony stood stock still, head down, its smoking sides heaving, the picture of exhaustion.

A humane man, Pettigrew reflected, would have dismounted at once, to give the animal a chance to recover. But he was not feeling in the least humane at the moment towards this beast, for a great many perfectly sound reasons. Besides, he had grave doubts whether in his present state, if he once got off its back, he would ever be able to get on again; and tired though he was of riding, the prospect of walking appealed to him now even less.

He looked around him. They were, he found, on a broad, level track, almost on the floor of the valley into which he had been looking from the heights above

49

such a short time before. The roaring in his ears
resolved itself into the sound of the stream, less than a
hundred yards away. Straight ahead of him he could
see what was evidently a ford. The track led directly
to it and on the other side ran parallel to the stream
until lost to sight in a wood—the same wood, he now
realized, as that into which the deer and its pursuers
had vanished not so long before. Then, quite suddenly,
as he watched, the scene, already vaguely familiar,
ceased to be anonymous. Place-names, long buried in
some hidden recesses of his brain, sprang to life. The
Ling Water, he told himself. And Martyrs Ford. Coney
Wood, and—down the valley out of sight—Coneywood
Mill, where he had seen his first stag killed.

It was a comfort to know exactly where he was,
because it helped him to determine what he was going
to do. Of one thing he was quite certain. He was not
going to try to return the way which he had come, even
supposing there was a practicable way back up the hill.
He had taken the pony on to Bolter's Tussock to look
for its rider. It was only too plain that he had found him.
After his recent experiences, it was easy to imagine how
that unfortunate came to be lying where he was. It was
only sheer luck—or the mercy of Heaven, according to
how you looked at it—that had saved him from becoming this horrible pony's second victim of the day.
But the discovery had left him with a certain obligation.
He could not, this time, simply ride away and say
nothing. Besides, he would have to explain his possession
of the pony to somebody, and the sooner the better.
He decided to be on his way at once. But which way?

A Check

While he hesitated, the pony settled the matter for him by suddenly coming to life and walking stiffly but purposefully towards the ford. Pettigrew was content to let it go. In that direction lay civilization, as represented by Coneywood Mill, and there was always the chance of falling in with the hunt before then. It was taking him away from Sallowcombe but that couldn't be helped. The problem of getting home must settle itself later on.

The pony walked half way across the ford and put its nose down into the water. Remembering a cautionary chapter in *Black Beauty*, Pettigrew tried to restrain it, but he might have been pulling at the bed of the river for all the difference that his efforts made. The beast slaked its thirst thoroughly and then consented to splash its way to the other side.

Once on the path again, the indomitable animal broke into a trot. Pettigrew, almost too weary to rise in the stirrups, let it jog on for what seemed an interminable distance on a very rough surface under trees with very low-hanging boughs. Presently the track was joined by another, larger path which came down the hill through the woods on their right. Evidently this was the way that the body of the hunt had come, for the imprints of their hooves were everywhere. The pony seemed to notice it also, for it lengthened its stride, making a gait already uncomfortable almost insupportable. Clearly it was as anxious for the company of its kind as Pettigrew himself. He was thankful when rounding a bend, he saw a man on horseback just ahead of him, moving at walking pace in the same direction.

A Check

The pony consented to slow down as they approached and signalled their presence by bumping heavily into the stranger's hindquarters. The rider looked round. He was evidently a native and not a visitor, which was all to the good. Pettigrew wasted no time in apologizing.

"I want your help," he said crisply. "There's a man been killed up on the moor, and I'm on his pony."

"Eh?"

The man was evidently very deaf. He had also, Pettigrew now observed, an absolutely villainous face.

"Eh?"

It is not easy to shout when one is as pumped as Pettigrew was, but he did his best.

"There's a man been killed," he bellowed. "*Killed!*"

The stranger gave a sudden hideous grin of comprehension.

"Killed!" he said. "Oh, ay—they'm killed all right, I reckon. Down to Coneywood Mill, I shouldn't wonder. You'd best hurry!"

A stout stick descended with a crack just behind the pony's saddle, and Pettigrew was carried helplessly away down the path at a smart canter, pursued by contemptuous laughter.

Fortunately for Pettigrew, who felt that by now he had plumbed the depths of humiliation, his mount soon began to show that its stamina was not after all quite inexhaustible. It was the best part of a mile to Coneywood Mill, and before that distance had been covered the canter had been reduced to a rather weary and perfectly manageable trot.

The fellow had been right. They had certainly killed.

52

A Check

Pettigrew pulled up to find himself at a scene which had not altered in essentials since he had been ceremonially blooded at the same spot all those years ago. In the little meadow that here separated the wood from the stream a close knot of interested spectators marked where no doubt the huntsman was breaking up his deer. A short distance away the pack was impatiently awaiting the remarkably unattractive portion of the carcase that would shortly fall to its share. And all around, the members of the field, for the most part dismounted, ate their sandwiches, sipped at their flasks, lit their pipes, and explained to one another how singularly well they had gone that day.

Pettigrew pushed his way on to the grass and looked round him, feeling suddenly at a loss. He had come there to report a violent death, and now he could see nobody to whom to report it. His immediate neighbour, a stout, self-satisfied young man, was holding a horse a good deal better bred than himself while he explained in penetrating tones exactly what had been wrong with the huntsman's tactics. Neither he nor the sharp-featured girl to whom he was talking looked as though they would be in the least interested in the information. Pettigrew moved on and passed in succession three small girls in jodhpurs giggling in a group, an extremely handsome young woman who was running her hands down her horse's off hind leg while addressing the creature in quite startlingly foul language, and two earnest young sportsmen who proved to be in anxious colloquy about the forthcoming ballet season. None of them seemed to Pettigrew appropriate recipients of his news. He glanced round at the pedestrian onlookers. Although quite a small crowd had collected, for once it did not include a policeman. None of the others stood out as the type of person to whom one should confide a delicate matter of this kind.

It was an altogether absurd situation. After having endured so much to arrive at Coneywood Mill, he seemed to be still as far from his objective as ever. Short of making an exhibition of himself by shouting out his story at the top of his voice, he did not see what he could do. To whom should one refer the news of a casualty occurring during a day's hunting? The Master of Hounds? Probably that was the right answer. After all, this was his hunt and he was in a way responsible. Pettigrew looked about for a commanding figure in pink coat and velvet cap and was relieved not to see him. A deeply conventional man, he felt that he was at the moment in no fit state to accost so important a functionary as the Master. It would be like going into Court without a wig. Even by modern standards, both he and his mount must look appallingly dishevelled. People were staring at them already.

One man was staring, at all events. And not only staring, but speaking.

"Here, you!" he said. "What are you doing on that pony?"

"Is this your pony?" said Pettigrew. "Thank God!"

He was a tall, heavy man riding a dun cob and he listened to the story with an impassive face. Pettigrew noticed that while it was being told he was looking, not at him but at the pony. When it was finished he

54

said, "And which of you let the pony down—you or him?"

Pettigrew murmured something to the effect that he wasn't sure.

"Dammit!" said the stranger. "Have you looked at his knees?"

Pettigrew had not looked at the pony's knees. He made up his mind there and then that he would avoid doing so if possible.

"Well," the man went on, briskly, "what have you done about this? Have you told Mr. Olding?"

"No," said Pettigrew, rather sulkily. "I have not. And who is Mr. Olding, anyway?"

"Who is he? Good God, don't you know anything? The Hunt Secretary, of course. I reckon this is his job if it's anyone's."

Why didn't I think of that? Pettigrew asked himself. Of course there is a secretary, and of course this is his job. Everything is. Blessed be the name of secretary. Amen.

"Mr. Olding! Mr. Olding, sir! Can you come here a minute?"

Mr. Olding could and did. He was a wiry, middle-aged man with keen eyes and that expression of resigned tolerance for human folly, common to senior police officers and hunt secretaries.

"Well, Tom, what is it this time?" he asked.

"Mr. Olding, sir, it's Mr. Percy. He's been thrown on Bolter's Tussock, and killed. This gentleman found him there, dead as mutton, and the pony with him. So he gets on the pony and rides down here to tell us."

Pettigrew was so impressed that even in his then

condition he should be described as a gentleman, that he scarcely noticed the inaccuracy of this account of his adventures.

"Very good of him," said Mr. Olding. He turned to Pettigrew. "I suppose you know that pony's got a shoe loose behind? I noticed it when you came through the gate just now."

"I—er——" said Pettigrew.

"I don't blame you. You must have had rather a rough ride coming down here."

"I allus told Mr. Percy he couldn't hold the pony," said Tom. "But he would have 'm."

"I suppose that's why you let him have the animal with a plain snaffle—just to make sure you'd be proved right. It's simply asking him to bolt."

"But he's not a bolter, Mr. Olding—you know that. It's simply that when he hears hounds——"

"All right, Tom. We won't waste time arguing. We'd better get back to poor Percy. Not that there'll be much we can do for him now." He led the way out of the field, talking over his shoulder as he went. "I shall have to break the news to his sister, I suppose. Do you know if she's got on the telephone yet, Tom? I must remember to ask her if she'll let me have that spaniel of Percy's. I was only talking to him about it the other day. He was due to shoot with me next week, and I said to him . . ."

Mr. Olding hit off a route back to Bolter's Tussock that was little longer and a great deal easier than the way by which Pettigrew had come down. None the less, Pettigrew found it a very exhausting ride. He was by now extremely stiff. His legs, in their unsuitable thin flannel trousers, felt lacerated. He had arrived at Coneywood Mill bathed in sweat and the fresh breeze which sprang up as they emerged from the wood sent a chill right through him. The pony went quietly enough, and for this he was grateful. He felt that in his then condition he was liable to tumble off its back on the slightest pretext.

"Well," said Mr. Olding, drawing rein on the heathery top of the Tussock. "Here we are. Where does he lie?"

Pettigrew had never prided himself on possessing a bump of direction, and he had wondered in the course of the ride whether he would be able to find the spot again without long search. But he need not have worried. The position was quite unmistakable. The road on one side and a conspicuous outcrop of rock on the other fixed it beyond doubt. He led the others to it without hesitation.

There was nothing there.

After what seemed a long time, Pettigrew heard Mr. Olding say, "It looks as if you'd made a mistake."

Pettigrew shook his head miserably.

"No," he said. "I'm not mistaken. This was the place all right."

"You're quite sure? You know what it is with a fallen bird. Unless you've marked it properly, you may be yards out when you go to pick it up."

Pettigrew did not know what it was with a fallen bird, but he remained positive.

A Check

"Well, in that case . . ." Mr. Olding turned to look at the pony's owner, and Pettigrew could see in his face a look of scepticism. "It's a rum business. What do you think, Tom?"

"Perhaps Mr. Percy wasn't all that dead, sir?" Tom suggested. "He'd only have a couple of yards to walk to the road, and he would have got a lift home from there."

"H'm. A runner, and not a dead bird? It's an idea."

"No," said Pettigrew. "When I saw him, he wasn't in a condition to walk a couple of yards, or any distance. And I'm pretty sure he never will be."

"You seem bloody positive about everything, sir," said Mr. Olding. "Upon my word, I'm beginning to wonder——"

"Mr. Olding, sir! Look behind you!" cried Tom.

They looked round. Advancing towards them from the direction of Tucker's Barrows was a small man in riding kit. His bowler hat had a dent in the crown, his face was flushed crimson with heat or emotion or both and he walked as a man will walk who has trudged some distance on a hot day, through thick heather, in top boots; but in all other respects he seemed to be perfectly hale, if not hearty.

"Good God! Percy!" exclaimed Mr. Olding.

CHAPTER VI

At Fault

"Are you all right, Percy?" asked Mr. Olding anxiously.

Percy said nothing for a moment. He stood there, in the centre of the little group of mounted men, his red face twitching, his breath coming and going.

"Am I all right?" he burst out finally. "My godfathers! What the hell do you expect me to be? All right! I like that!"

He broke into what was evidently intended to be derisive laughter, but which turned into a fit of coughing.

"This gentleman said you was dead," said Tom.

"This *gentleman*," bellowed Percy, "stole my horse."

"I did nothing of the sort," Pettigrew protested.

"If you didn't, I'd like to know what you're doing on him now."

"That at least is easily remedied," said Pettigrew in as dignified a tone as he could summon up. With an immense effort he lifted a leg which felt like solid wood over the pony's back and got down to the ground.

"Thank you," said Percy in a voice heavy with sarcasm and took the pony's reins.

Pettigrew was about to say something further, but it

59

was clear that for the time being any words would be wasted on Percy. He was fully occupied in trying to get into the saddle. Quite evidently, the pony, which had been meekness itself when Pettigrew mounted it, had a personal dislike to Percy. No sooner was his foot in the stirrup than it began a rapid circular movement with its forelegs for centre and its hindquarters for circumference, leaving a blaspheming Percy to hop uncomfortably after it. Olding came up alongside in an endeavour to help, but his own horse, hitherto perfectly staid, immediately began to plunge and rear, finishing the performance by kicking the pony smartly in the ribs. The spectacle came to an end only when Tom, who had dismounted, walked across and held the pony firmly by the bridle. It should have been funny, Pettigrew reflected, but he was beyond being amused. He could not even muster a smile at the spectacle of Percy, at last in the saddle, trying to control a restive animal with one hand while shortening his stirrup leathers with the other. Everything that had happened since he began his fatal walk towards Bolter's Tussock had been so completely alien to what he normally knew as real life that he began to wonder whether the whole thing was not a bad dream. Only the aches and pains that now possessed his every limb were actual enough.

"Stole my horse!" Percy repeated. After manœuvres covering about half an acre of moor he had at last got his mount and tackle under control. "Damn it, I saw him in the act."

"Did you, by Jove!" said Mr. Olding. "Why didn't you stop him?"

At Fault

"Stop him? Look here, I came down just this side of Tucker's Barrows—the bloody pony got away with me and put his foot in a peat cutting if you want to know. All right. He went on, across the Tussock, just as I knew he would, making for home. Right, Tom?"

"Yassur. He allus does."

"All right. I knew I'd pick him up at the gate to your field, if not sooner. So I followed on. Right?"

Mr. Olding gravely nodded. Clearly it was all right by him.

"Then the next thing I know, here's this fellow on the pony, cantering across the top as though the whole place belonged to him. I shouted at him—I waved— and what does he do? Turns round like a flash and rides lickety split down hill as hard as he can go after the hounds. All right. If that isn't stealing I'd like to know what is."

"*A person steals who, without the consent of the owner . . .*" As a pious man in extremity will say a prayer, so Pettigrew murmured to himself the opening words of the Larceny Act, 1916. The familiar phrases comforted him. Not only did they assure him of his own innocence in law; they represented something solid and substantial to cling to at a moment when he was beginning to doubt the evidence of his senses. He had got to the stage of feeling that if the others went on discussing him as though he wasn't there, he would soon begin to question his own identity.

"And then," Olding was saying, "he turns up at the kill with a cock-and-bull story about finding your bleeding carcase with the pony standing over it."

61

"All right. That proves it, doesn't it?"

"Oh, rather, I should say it did."

"*. . . fraudulently and without a claim of right made in good faith . . .*"

"You'll give evidence about it, if they want you to?"

"Oh, I say, Percy, that's going a bit far, isn't it? I mean, that sort of thing isn't going to do the Hunt any good, and you've got the pony back."

"All right, if you say so, Olding. It seems a pity to let the blighter off scot free, though. What I can't get over is his saying I was dead. Such blasted cheek."

"*. . . takes and carries away anything capable of being stolen . . .*"

"He went on saying it right up to the end. Took me to the very place where he said you'd be. I was led right up the garden path. Absolutely, I can tell you."

"Extraordinary thing to do. Do you think he's quite——?"

For the first time the two men seemed to be aware that Pettigrew was listening to their conversation. They did not stop talking, but walked their mounts out of earshot.

"*. . . with intent, at the time of such taking, permanently to deprive the owner thereof,*" Pettigrew concluded defiantly. Let anyone suggest he was out of his mind after that!

"Did you say something, sir?"

He looked round. Tom was speaking to him, and speaking, moreover, in a surprisingly friendly tone. Moreover, he was standing at Pettigrew's elbow and not talking down at him from the vantage point of a saddle.

The fact encouraged Pettigrew to treat him as a man and a brother. At the same time it puzzled him.

"What have you done to your horse?" he asked.

Tom grinned, and jerked his thumb over his shoulder. Looking past him, Pettigrew saw the horse standing where Tom had left it when he dismounted to help Percy. It was quite motionless, its head up, its ears pricked, looking towards its master as though waiting for orders.

"That's a well-trained animal," said Pettigrew. "Better behaved than your pony," he added with a feeble laugh.

"I can't afford a disobedient animal in *my* job," Tom replied. "He'll stay there all day if I tell him to, *and* come when he's called."

Tired as he was, Pettigrew looked with interest at this equine phenomenon. He was no judge of horseflesh, but he thought it a very plain-looking animal, a stocky dun-coloured beast, with powerful quarters and a distinctly roman nose. He approached it and its ears went flat back on its head while a set of very ugly teeth champed in his direction.

"Don't go too close," Tom called out. "He's not safe with strangers."

Pettigrew turned back. Tom was vaguely poking about in the heather with his hunting-crop, a look of scepticism on his face.

"Somewhere about here, you thought he was?" he asked.

"Yes," said Pettigrew. "I don't know whether you think me mad or not, but there was a man lying here."

63

Tom nodded gravely. "'Twasn't Mr. Percy, though," he remarked.

"Obviously not, if he came down at Tucker's Barrows. It was someone else."

"And he's not there now."

"And he's not there now. That's what's so extraordinary."

"What did he look like, exactly?" Tom asked.

Pettigrew closed his eyes for a moment, the better to concentrate. The picture that he saw in his mind's eye was absolutely clear. The man was lying on his back, his head slightly askew on the narrow shoulders, the face upturned, looking very white and sharp against the ground, like a piece of paper. The pony all but trod on him, so that Pettigrew was thrown forward and only saved himself from falling by holding on to his mane. . . .

He suddenly realized something, and with the realization his head began to swim. Tom's pony had a severely hogged mane. Nobody could possibly have held on to that. He was confusing it with the far smaller pony that he had ridden as a boy, which had sported a long, flowing chestnut mane. And the dead face that he had just been seeing so clearly in his mind's eye was part of the same vivid memory. He must think again. But try as he might, he could not summon up any precise picture of what he had seen that afternoon. The whole episode was hopelessly blurred in his mind.

He shook his head.

"I'm afraid I can't say what he looked like," he said lamely.

"But you saw him?"

"Oh yes. I saw him all right."

"Ah." Tom said nothing more for an appreciable time. "A funny old place, the Tussock," he remarked at last. "There's no knowing what you mightn't see up here. Night times, especially. Of course, there is those as can see by day."

"Do you mean the place is—haunted?"

Tom shrugged his shoulders.

"I'm not saying it is," he said. "But there's them as do."

"But that's ridiculous," Pettigrew protested. But even as he spoke, doubts assailed him. After all, the Tussock *was* haunted for him, and in a very particular way. The conditions for a hallucination were ideal. He had been all day obsessed with the recollections of the past, of which this one, because so long suppressed, had become by far the most powerful. Given the coincidence of the pony's sudden swerve at precisely the right time and place to fit in with his thoughts, was it not possible that an optical illusion might follow? And people who were prone to optical illusions of this nature might be called, as Percy put it, "not quite . . ."

He felt strongly the necessity of impressing upon someone his sanity and respectability, if only to convince himself that he was, in spite of everything, sane and respectable. "I'm afraid I may have done your pony some damage," he went on quickly. "If you think you ought to call in a vet, you must do it at my expense. There'll be the shoeing to pay for anyway, and I dare say you feel I ought to give you something for my ride."

At Fault

Tom looked at him seriously and not unkindly. "That's a fair offer, sir," he said. "I tell you what— you've not got a bad seat on a horse—better than Mr. Percy's, if you want to know. What do you say if I was to find you something a bit quieter, more suitable to a man of your age, like? I'd forget about the other matter then. What do you say?"

Pettigrew shook his head.

"No," he said. "Thank you for the compliment but quite definitely No."

Tom shrugged his shoulders and looked round to where the other two men were now approaching. Then he gave a whistle, and his horse trotted obediently up to where he stood. He climbed easily into the saddle. "Shall I let you know about the pony, then?" he asked.

"Do, please. My name is Pettigrew and I am staying at Sallowcombe."

"Oh." The friendliness in the man's face faded as the colour in a Japanese lantern fades when the candle inside is blown out. He turned his horse's head away. "Well, Mr. Olding," he called out, "we'd best be getting along home."

Pettigrew stared after the three men as they rode away across the moor in a mood of gloomy resignation. He was too tired even to feel resentment at the brutally sudden change of front. It seemed, in any case, all of a piece with the illogical sequence of disasters that had marked the afternoon. No doubt there was an explanation, but it was not worth while looking for one. Just now he was concerned only with how he, Pettigrew, was to get along home from where he was.

66

At Fault

The sound of motor traffic close at hand reminded him that Bolter's Tussock was no longer the remote spot that it once had been. He moved wearily but thankfully towards the road.

The first vehicle that approached him pulled up at his frantic signals. With an extraordinary sense of returning to reality from a world of dreams, he opened the door and climbed in beside his wife.

"Frank, darling!" she exclaimed. "What have you been up to now?"

But Frank was already fast asleep.

CHAPTER VII

Lying Up

"I think," said Eleanor, "that it might be a good plan if you were to go to bed."

Her husband murmured faintly that perhaps it would. He was far too grateful to her for the superb tact with which she had refrained from asking any questions about his afternoon's adventures to oppose any suggestion that she might care to make. But in any case he knew that the sooner he was in bed the better. It was not merely that he was extremely tired; he felt, if not ill, at least decidedly out of sorts. The appetite which he had brought home from his expedition had dwindled to nothing at the sight of food, and from certain uneasy qualms he was fairly sure that he was running a temperature. This latter fact, however, he hoped would escape Eleanor's notice.

Vain hope! No sooner was he in bed than a thermometer was thrust into his mouth. Following the maddening custom of nurses all the world over, Eleanor did not reveal the verdict, but he was not interested in the precise reading. He knew without being told that he was officially an invalid. He knew, further, that he had brought it on himself, and that it served him right. He

68

swallowed meekly the concoction that Eleanor handed him and sank gratefully back on his pillow.

His sleep was restless and disturbed by ugly dreams. Waking in the small hours, he was shocked to realize that they were in all essentials the same grisly nightmares that had troubled him as a schoolboy, with perhaps an added element of horror. If he had not realized it before, he knew now that the sentimental backward journey in time on which he had been engaged had its dangers as well as its attractions. I must be my age in future, he told himself, and on that resolution fell asleep once more.

Whether because his resolution took effect or for some other cause, his sleep this time was peaceful enough. He woke late, his fever gone, but with a body aching as though it had been scientifically belaboured by experts. He accepted without protest the decision that he should spend the day in bed. An immense lassitude of mind possessed him. He was vaguely conscious of there being something that should be done, a decision that ought to be taken, but he drowsily postponed the effort of even seeking to remember what it was.

It was Sunday morning. Eleanor had announced her intention of going to church for morning service. Sunday newspapers came late to this remote spot, but he had brought plenty of books with him, and presently he roused himself sufficiently to glance at them. He picked up successively a historical work which he was very anxious to read, a neglected classic which he had always intended to read and a cheap thriller which he had brought along because Eleanor liked that sort of stuff.

Lying Up

One hour, eight chapters and one hundred and twenty
pages later, he was contemplating the predicament of a
heroine who owed her perilous state entirely to her pig-
headed refusal to inform the proper authorities that in
Chapter I she had found a dead body in her dustbin.
Pettigrew felt that this was trying his credibility a little
too high. At the same time, the young woman's dilemma
seemed in some way faintly familiar. . . . His tired brain
shied away from the problem that lay just below the
level of consciousness, and by the time that Eleanor returned from church he was slumbering once more.

He made only a pretence of eating lunch, and the
tray was hardly out of the room before he was again
asleep. Some time later he was jerked wide awake by the
ringing of a bell. It took him an appreciable time to
realize that it was a telephone, and that the thudding
sounds that made his bed shake were the footsteps of
Mrs. Gorman scurrying to answer it. It still seemed to
him vaguely inappropriate that Sallowcombe should
have this, or any other, attribute of modernity. Evidently, the line was not particularly good, for Mrs.
Gorman's part in the conversation was loud enough to
penetrate all over the house. Pettigrew could not but
hear, though at first he paid little attention to what was
being said. He caught the name of "Gilbert" repeated
once or twice, and then, "When did it happen?" He
was left in no doubt as to what had happened to Gilbert,
for Mrs. Gorman's next words were: "Well, it's a merci-
ful release, I reckon, after all these years." The phrase
struck Pettigrew as being neither original nor provoca-
tive, but it was plainly not to the taste of the other party

to the conversation, for Mrs. Gorman's succeeding observation, spoken very loudly and with an unexpected rasp in her voice, was: "I'll thank you not to talk to me like that, Louisa. You can keep that sort of language for Jack. If you dare to use it, that is."

By this time, Pettigrew was unashamedly listening to what promised to be an exciting family row. But it did not develop in the way that might have been expected. "What?" Mrs. Gorman went on, "What did you say? ... No, of course not. Jack isn't with me at this moment, you know that as well as I do. . . . Well, I don't know, I'm sure . . . He's his own master, I suppose . . . Yes, he'll be at the funeral, miss, and the girls too. At Minster, of course. Tuesday? Wednesday? . . . You'll let me know. Very well." And she rang off.

There succeeded a full half minute of dead silence, before Pettigrew heard Mrs. Gorman's footsteps moving away from the entrance hall where the telephone was situated. Pettigrew pictured her standing quietly there, turning over in her mind the significance of what she had just heard. To judge from the tone of her voice, the question of Jack's whereabouts had caused her a good deal more concern than Gilbert's death. It was tantalizing to find oneself on the fringe of a domestic drama, with no obvious means of penetrating any nearer to its centre. He would have liked to discuss it with Eleanor, but at his express desire, she had taken herself off on to the moor for the afternoon, rather than waste the fine weather with him indoors. Now his watch told him that it was nearly time for tea, and he realized with pleasure that he was looking forward to it with something

71

approaching hunger. He heard the front door of the house open and close again and a little later Mr. Joliffe's deep, slow voice. Evidently his daughter came to meet him in the hall, for her voice mingled with his. The voices moved in the direction of Mr. Joliffe's sitting-room and the door shut with a bang. Half an hour later he was still waiting for his tea in a mood of starved exasperation. It was all very well for Mrs. Gorman to discuss with her father the news of Gilbert's death, but she had no business to allow such personal matters to come before her duty to her guests. People had no sense of obligation nowadays. . . .

The door of the sitting-room must have opened, for he suddenly heard a babel of words. Mrs. Gorman and her father were both talking at once, and talking in no very friendly spirit, to judge from the tone of their voices. Of what they said, Pettigrew could distinguish one word only, which was repeated by both speakers with considerable emphasis. It was the name, "Jack". Once more, he observed, it was the live Jack rather than the deceased Gilbert who seemed to be the centre of concern. Then he heard the sitting-room door close again, and Mrs. Gorman's footsteps making their way across the hall and along the passage that led to the kitchen. He thought, too, that he could distinguish something very much like a sob.

The tea was brought after what in the circumstances Pettigrew could not but feel was a commendably short interval. It was a tea worth waiting for, in the true Exmoor tradition, with farmhouse scones, heather honey in the comb and clotted cream. It was brought, not by Mrs. Gorman but by Doreen, breathing heavily and biting her underlip as she manœuvred the tray into position, with Beryl, her younger sister, in giggling attendance.

"Mum says she's sorry she can't bring the tea herself, but she's a bit upset this afternoon," said Doreen gravely.

"I'm sorry," said Pettigrew, politely.

"Uncle Gilbert's dead!" exclaimed Beryl from the door, in a tone that was more like a shout of triumph than anything else.

"You be quiet, Beryl!" Doreen commanded. "It's quite true what she says," she informed Pettigrew. "But he wasn't a real uncle, only a sort of cousin."

"I see," said Pettigrew. "I'm sorry."

"There isn't nothing to be sorry about," remarked Doreen coldly. "Uncle Gilbert's been ill for ages and ages. And now he's dead we shall get all his money, Mummy says."

"And we shall all go away and live with Daddy and leave the 'lectric light on as much as we like," chanted Beryl. "All day if we want to. And I shall have a bicycle and a——"

"That's enough!" Doreen drove her sister from the room, and turned back to Pettigrew. "You'll have to excuse Beryl," she said. "Mum's always on at her about gossiping to strangers, but she's that young, she will do it. And Mum says if there's anything else you require will you knock on the floor and I'll come up."

Pettigrew required nothing else except some further information to satisfy his curiosity about the Gorman family, and this was denied him. Doreen had gone some way to clear up the question of Gilbert's identity, and he knew from Eleanor that Jack was identical with the Daddy who was expected to allow his daughters to leave the electric light on—a sidelight on Jack's character which he had not expected. But this still left a number of questions unanswered. Pettigrew postponed their consideration until he had disposed of his tea. Eating clotted cream and honey in bed may be among the highest of human pleasures, but it demands from its votaries undivided attention if it is to be accomplished without disaster to the bed-clothes. The tray removed (by a subdued and silent Mrs. Gorman), he pondered at length the various problems raised by the evidence, and amused himself by fabricating a number of theories to account for them. Then Eleanor came in, and with her assistance the theories became progressively more and more fantastic. It was merely idle curiosity on his part. The affairs of the Gormans and their congeners could be of no conceivable interest to him. But it served to pass the time—served, too, as an excuse for shelving once more the question which, at the back of his mind, he knew would have to be faced sooner or later.

He slept badly again that night.

CHAPTER VIII

An Old Friend

On Monday morning Eleanor found it necessary to go into Whitsea to shop, and after the usual business with the thermometer decreed that her husband was to stay in bed until the afternoon, when he might get up. Once more Pettigrew was left to his own devices. He demanded nothing better. It was just the opportunity he needed for some serious reading. . . .

Despite the heroine's initial absurdity, the thriller really turned out very well. Pettigrew laid it down at last with a satisfied smile. He had guessed the criminal correctly, though admittedly for the wrong reasons. He leaned back on his pillow and stared out of the window at the familiar shapes of Tucker's Barrows, dark on the horizon. He had not the energy to start another, heavier book. He was not in the least sleepy. There was still some time to go before lunch. He had nothing now to divert his mind from the problem which more or less unconsciously he had been shirking ever since his wife had rescued him by the road side. Was he to go to the police with the story of what he had seen on Bolter's Tussock, and if so, what was that story to be?

The mood of fantasy in which he had been living two days before had deserted him entirely. In his sober

75

senses he was quite certain that he had seen what he
took to be the body of a man at a particular spot, and
that it had not been there on his return, perhaps three
quarters of an hour later. His duty as a citizen was perfectly plain. But even as he made the resolution, he
realized what it would be like endeavouring to explain
to a polite but sceptical police sergeant exactly what he
had done on that occasion, and why; he heard, as
though he were present, the comments of Messrs. Olding and Percy when called upon—as assuredly they
would be called upon—to make their statements to the
officer charged with the enquiry; he saw himself labelled
as a half-witted busybody sent by providence to plague
a hard-worked police force; and he wondered whether
his duty as a citizen really involved him in all this. After
all, he had seen whatever it was that he had seen for a
very short time. He was in a highly suggestible state
just then. Without admitting any truth to the man
Tom's ridiculous theory, there was always the possibility that he might have been mistaken. And if it
turned out that he had been, then he would simply have
exposed himself to ridicule to no purpose. The temptation to save himself from all this by simply doing
nothing was almost irresistible; but some stubborn element in him resisted none the less.

The conflict was still unresolved when Eleanor returned.

"You're looking much better," she assured him.

"I am much better."

"Well enough to eat lunch?"

"Quite well enough to eat lunch."

An Old Friend

"Well enough to receive a visitor?"

"That depends on the visitor," said Pettigrew warily. "If it is the girl friend at Minster Tracy——"

"No, it's not the girl friend." Eleanor called over her shoulder down the stairs, "Do come up!" Then she said, "I'm leaving you together," and disappeared.

Pettigrew began to say something, but his protest died on his lips as the open doorway was blocked by the appearance of a broad, bulky figure—a figure, once agreeably familiar, that he had not seen for more than ten years, and which now seemed broader, bulkier and more agreeable than ever.

"Inspector Mallett!" Pettigrew exclaimed. "This is a pleasure!"

"Not Inspector," said Mallett. "Plain Mister. I retired after the war, with the rank of Superintendent. I thought you knew," he added reproachfully.

He walked across the room with the almost silent tread that always seemed so remarkable in a man of his enormous size and sat down by the bedside. Pettigrew looked into his wide, honest, intelligent face with something approaching affection.

"Do you know," he said, "I haven't thought of you for years, but now you are here I believe you're the very man I've been waiting to see."

"That," said Mallett, "seemed to be the opinion of your good lady when I met her in Whitsea this morning."

Pettigrew could find nothing better to say than, "Oh."

"Perhaps I shouldn't have said that," Mallett observed.

77

"I'm sorry, but one loses one's finesse, living in the country."

"Don't apologize," murmured Pettigrew. "I was just wondering how my good lady knew, that was all."

"I'm never surprised at anything ladies know and by very few things ladies do," was the reply. "Do you remember, Mr. Pettigrew——?"

They remembered in good earnest for some time. Then Pettigrew said:

"And what made you retire to this part of the world, Mr. Mallett?"

"It was my good lady's wish, sir. She came from Exmoor. And now that I'm unhappily a widower, I stay on from force of habit. It's quiet, but I don't complain. My hobby keeps me busy."

"Your hobby? What is that? Bee-keeping or rose-growing?"

"Neither, sir, thank you for the compliment. I leave bee-keeping to Sherlock Holmes. And rose-growing— let me see—that was Sergeant Cuff, wasn't it?"

"You study the detective classics, I see."

"Not the classics only, Mr. Pettigrew. Detective fiction of all sorts. This is the hobby I was talking about. I'm writing a book about it. What you might call a treatise—from the professional point of view. Coming to the subject fresh, as I did, I found it full of surprises."

"I suppose surprise is what the authors are after."

"Not that sort of surprise only, sir. It's the way that some of their characters behave that surprises me. Take that book on your bed now, for example. What would you think of anyone in real life finding a corpse in their

78

dustbin and not saying a word about it to the police? Surprising isn't the word for it. It's ridiculous, isn't it?"

"Quite," said Pettigrew. "Quite. I was thinking the same thing myself. All the same, there may be circumstances when—— Look here, Mallett, I'd rather like your advice about this . . ."

And as Mallett leant forward to hear what he had to say, he had the strongest possible impression that this was precisely what his visitor had come for.

"Yes," Mallett was saying thoughtfully, "Yes." He tugged at the ends of his grizzled moustache in a well-remembered gesture. "And this body—appearance—ghost—whatever you like to call it—looked like what, exactly?"

"That was what Tom asked me."

"And you couldn't tell him, because your head was too full of what happened when you were a nipper. I know. But your head's clear now. What do you say it looked like, *now*?"

"I've only a very vague recollection, you know. I didn't see it for more than a second or two. It's difficult to say."

"Try."

Under the influence of that calm, compelling tone, Pettigrew tried.

"Flannel trousers and a bluey-grey coat," he said at last. "Open-necked shirt—white or pale yellow."

"Hat?"

"No hat."

"Hair, then."

79

An Old Friend

"Lightish brown—there might have been a bit of a curl in it." ·

"What else?"

"Nothing else. I couldn't see the face. I'm afraid this is all too indefinite to be much use."

"On the contrary, it's very definite, and very useful. It proves one thing, that whatever you saw on Bolter's Tussock yesterday, it wasn't the ghost of the man you saw there fifty years ago. I don't know how *he* was dressed, but I bet he wasn't wearing flannel trousers and an open-necked shirt. Breeches and stockings and a collar and tie, more likely. "

"Of course," said Pettigrew. He began to laugh. "How ridiculously obvious! Why didn't I think of that before?"

"Well," said Mallett tolerantly, "you had other things to think of, no doubt. That's one possibility out of the way, anyhow."

"Did you ever consider it a serious possibility?"

Mallett shrugged his great shoulders.

"More things in heaven and earth, you know," he said. "But I shouldn't have expected it from *you*, Mr. Pettigrew."

"I don't know whether that is a compliment or not. Let's think about other possibilities."

"Well, sir, the next possibility is that the man you saw was simply a hiker asleep on the grass, and that while you were gone he just got up and walked away. What do you think of that?"

"Not very much. It's difficult to say why, exactly, but——"

"I know. Nothing so stiff as a stiff."

"It's more likely, if I was mistaken, that what I saw wasn't a man at all, but just a chance combination of stones and grasses and so on that gave the impression of someone lying there. All the same, I don't believe it. The question is, would the police believe it?"

Mallett did not answer the question. Instead, he asked another. "Has it occurred to you, Mr. Pettigrew," he said, "that a body doesn't get to and from a place like this without someone putting it there and taking it away again, and that anyone carting corpses about is apt to leave traces?"

"Of course," said Pettigrew. "But the day before yesterday I had hardly the chance——"

"Nobody's blaming you, sir. What I was getting at is this: supposing there is something here to go to the police about, there ought to be some proof of it on the spot. Wouldn't it be as well for you to go there again first thing to-morrow with someone—someone with a bit of experience, shall we say?—to check up first? If there's nothing there, the police aren't going to believe your yarn. If there is, then you can go straight off to the station and leave it to them to find the clues all over again for themselves."

"You mean, you'll come with me and look at the place yourself?"

"That was my idea."

"I am enormously obliged to you." Pettigrew felt relieved at thus disposing of his problem, and at the same time ashamed at shifting a burden that was properly his on to another's shoulders.

An Old Friend

"It's I'm obliged to you, sir. I shall enjoy it. It will be quite like old times. Besides, if anything comes of this, I shan't be at all sorry to score off Master Percy. Calling *you* a thief, Mr. Pettigrew! It's like his impudence. He's a proper pain in the neck, that fellow is."

"So you know him?"

"Naturally, I know him. And Mr. Olding too. I reckon to know everyone in these parts. Barring the visitors, there aren't so many of them."

"Then you can tell me—is Percy his christian name or his surname?"

"Both. Percy Percy. It's dreadful what some parents will do to their children, isn't it? Enough to give any boy a what-you-call-it complex."

"What about the man who owned the pony? I never found out his proper name. Is it Tom Tom, by any chance?"

"From your account that will be Tom Gorman. He has the farm at Highbarn. He has been acting as harbourer for the hunt this season, I believe."

"Harbourer—let me see if I can remember. He's the man whose job is to locate the whereabouts of a stag, of the proper size—a—what's the phrase?—a *warrantable* deer. So that they won't waste their time on females and small fry. He has to go out first thing in the morning, 'before the dawn is grey'. Does anyone read Whyte Melville's poetry nowadays, I wonder?"

"I couldn't say, sir."

"I remember wondering what he was when he told me that he needed an obedient horse for his job. Obviously he must have something that will stand still while he spies out the land. Well, that's Tom Gorman—an important functionary. I'd have treated him with more respect if I'd known. What connection is he to Mr. Joliffe's daughter?"

"When I said I knew these people, sir, I didn't mean I knew all about them. You'd have to be born and bred among them to do that. There's a lot of intermarriage, naturally, and frankly, all their relationships are beyond me. All I do know is that there's not much love lost between the families."

"That explains it. This man Tom was perfectly friendly until I mentioned that I was staying here, and then he shut up like a clam, and a very ugly clam at that. What was the trouble about?"

Mallett shook his head.

"It goes back a long way, I fancy," he said. "I believe it began with a dispute over a will. There's supposed to be money somewhere in the Gorman family, though Tom hasn't anything, and there's not much this end either. Have you met Jack Gorman, by the way?"

"Jack?"

"Your Mrs. Gorman's husband—Joliffe's son-in-law."

"No. My wife only heard of his existence on Saturday. Indeed, we'd taken it for granted till then that Mrs. Gorman was a widow."

"Oh, she's married, all right. They say she—but look here, Mr. Pettigrew, I mustn't waste any more time gossiping. I shall be late for lunch as it is, and my housekeeper won't be pleased. I'll be round to-morrow morning. Good-bye till then."

An Old Friend

"Did you have an interesting talk with Mr. Mallett about old times?" asked Eleanor, when she appeared with the tray for lunch.

"You didn't bring Mallett here to talk about old times," Pettigrew replied. "Now perhaps you'll tell me how he knew what I wanted to talk about."

"Well, dear," Eleanor said gently, "you had two rather disturbed nights, and you have taken lately to talking in your sleep . . ."

So it was as simple as that! Pettigrew reflected as he attacked his lunch.

CHAPTER IX

The Gathering of the Eagles

When he was small, Pettigrew used invariably to wake up early on hunting mornings. He would open his eyes to the early light of day with the consciousness that something extremely exciting and rather alarming was going to happen; and it would usually be some time before he was sufficiently wide awake to remember exactly what it was. On the morning succeeding Mallett's visit, he found himself experiencing much the same symptoms. This time, however, he beguiled his waking moments by reflections that would not have occurred to him then. In particular, he found himself listening for what had roused him three days before—the sound of feet scraping on a lead roof. Presently he heard, not what he was waiting for, but the footfalls of someone walking quietly across the farmyard. Pettigrew told himself firmly that he had no business to spy on the private affairs of other people, but none the less found himself a moment later peering out of window. He was rewarded by the sight of nothing more inspiring than Mr. Joliffe walking from his own back door to his own garage.

Feeling rather ashamed of his vulgar curiosity, Pettigrew was about to get back into bed when as ill luck would have it, Mr. Joliffe looked up and saw him. If he was surprised at the sight he did not allow it to shew on his serious features.

"Good morning, Mr. Pettigrew," he said politely.

"Good morning," answered Pettigrew, sincerely hoping that he would not wake Eleanor up. Then feeling that something more was demanded of him, he added rather pointlessly, "You're up early, I see."

Very gravely, Mr. Joliffe consulted his wrist-watch.

"I don't think so," he said. "A little before my usual time perhaps, but not much. There's a lot to do before a shop opens, Tuesday mornings especially, we being closed on Mondays. But I dare say it's early for *you*, Mr. Pettigrew. Were you looking for anything in particular?"

As Mr. Joliffe looked up at him with his expression of solemn enquiry, Pettigrew felt an insane desire to try the effect of saying, "I was looking to see whether a man would climb out of your daughter's window." But even as the thought passed through his mind, he wondered whether the remark would be such a shock to him after all. The eyes turned up in his direction were narrowed against the morning sun striking over the farmhouse roof. Perhaps it was this that gave an effect of slyness to the whole face which he had not seen there before. Whatever the reason, Pettigrew had the sudden feeling that there was some unacknowledged complicity between them.

"Don't catch cold, Mr. Pettigrew," said Mr. Joliffe quietly. "It's a fine morning, but sharp—sharp."

The Gathering of the Eagles

When Mallett drove up to the door of Sallowcombe, Eleanor surprised her husband by saying with unusual humility, "Would you mind very much if I came with you this morning?"

"Of course not," Pettigrew murmured, in a tone that any experienced wife could interpret as meaning that he would. He had taken it for granted that this expedition was to be a strictly masculine affair, though he would have been hard put to it to find any logical reason for the assumption. Perhaps it was that so far as Eleanor was concerned he felt, if not ashamed, at least extremely sensitive about the whole business. It had put him in an embarrassing and undignified situation, which as between husband and wife was better passed over in silence. It was far easier to discuss it with an outsider like Mallett, who would look at it in the cold light of the professional observer. But how to convey all this in the presence of a third party at the very moment of departure?

"If I may venture to say so," said Mallett, "I had rather taken it for granted that you would be of the party, madam. I have packed a snack for three."

On the back seat of Mallett's car, Pettigrew could see a vast picnic basket bulging at the seams. Remembering of old Mallett's reputation as a trencherman, he realized that his idea of a snack for three would be hopelessly beyond the capacity of any four normal persons. He submitted with what he hoped was a good grace.

There was not room for more than two in the front of the car, and Eleanor shared the back seat with the picnic basket. Her plea that there was more room for her husband's long legs in the seat beside the driver was perfectly true on the face of it, but the tactful way in which she thus indicated that her presence in the party was only on sufferance was not lost on Frank. It was, he reflected, characteristic of her that having captured the citadel she should allow the defeated garrison to march out with the full honours of war.

Once more, it was a beautiful day. The sun beat down between the high banks, crowned with beech hedges, that closed in the narrow road on either side. On just such a day Pettigrew could remember toiling on foot behind a wagonette drawn by two sweating horses up the incline which the car was now effortlessly climbing. He decided that in the interests of boys and beasts alike there was a lot to be said for progress after all. They overtook a police constable, pushing his bicycle up the hill, and sweating in his thick uniform almost as much as the horses had done; and he wished for his sake that progress could have gone a little further.

Mallett gave a friendly wave to the policeman as they passed, and then glanced at the clock on the dashboard before him. Pettigrew noticed a puzzled frown on his face.

"Is that clock right, Mr. Pettigrew?"

"I think so, yes. Is anything the matter?"

"Nothing the matter that I know of, sir. It's a little odd, that's all. Unless this clock's wrong, which you tell me it isn't, or unless the local Superintendent's altered his timetable, which I don't see why he should, that constable's three-quarters of an hour early on his beat."

The Gathering of the Eagles

"Oh," said Pettigrew, for want of anything better to say.

"If you mean by that, sir, that it's none of my business, I respectfully agree with you. It's just habit, noticing these things, and——"

They had reached the junction with the new main road, the presence of which on the moor had distressed Pettigrew so much three days before. As Mallett slowed down before turning to the right, in the direction of Bolter's Tussock, a car coming at great pace shot across their front from left to right. Mallett had to slam on his brakes abruptly to avoid a collision.

They took the corner soberly and followed up the slope behind the other car, now a hundred yards ahead and increasing its distance every moment. It vanished from their sight round the bend at the crest of the hill, beyond which the road levelled out to cross the comparatively flat Tussock.

"That fellow is in a bit of a hurry," observed Pettigrew.

Mallett said nothing, but the frown had returned to his face and he took one hand off the steering wheel to administer a tremendous tug to the end of his moustache. About fifty yards below the top of the hill, he seemed to come to a decision. He slowed down, changed into low gear and swung left-handed off the highway onto a narrow, rutted track which came into the road at that point.

The car bucketed violently on the rough surface. Pettigrew, Eleanor and the picnic basket were flung from side to side as Mallett remorselessly drove his car onwards and upwards across the flank of the hill on a course more or less parallel with the road below them. Then, at a comparatively level spot, he stopped the car and switched off the engine.

Pettigrew was the first to speak.

"I thought we were going to Bolter's Tussock," he said in an aggrieved tone.

"So we are, I hope, in a minute or two," said Mallett. "It's just an idea I've got, Mr. Pettigrew, if you'll excuse me. Do you see anything down there?"

From the windows of the car there was a good deal to be seen "down there"—a large slice of Exmoor, the whole width of the Bristol Channel and several miles of the coast of Wales. The one thing that was invisible from this particular point was the part of Bolter's Tussock for which they had been making, as it was hidden from them by the bank lining the road immediately beneath their position. Pettigrew said as much, and Mallett nodded placidly.

"Just so," he said. "Just so. But we can see the road where it leaves the Tussock to go down the hill. You can follow it half the way to Whitsea. Do you see anything on that?"

"Yes," said Pettigrew. "There's a bus, or a coach—I'm not sure which—and a motor bicycle overtaking it."

"Quite right, sir. The coach coming back from taking the children into school at Whitsea. And a motor bike, as you say. Both coming up to meet us. But nothing going our way—away from us, I mean?"

"No."

The Gathering of the Eagles

Mallett sighed.

"I was afraid so," he said.

It was Eleanor who saw the point first.

"That car in front of us," she said. "It ought to be somewhere down the road by now. We should be bound to get a view of it if it had gone on. It must have stopped on the Tussock."

"Just so, madam."

"All the same," said Pettigrew, "I don't see why——"

"It's the divisional detective inspector's private car, sir. With the inspector in it." He looked back along the way they had come. "And here comes the constable on his bike," he added. "He's made pretty good time up the hill. What do you make of that, Mr. Pettigrew?"

"I'm reminded of a text from the Bible," said Pettigrew.

"And that is——"

"Do you mind awfully if I don't tell you just now? I have a feeling it would be unlucky. Can't we try to find out what this high-powered policeman is up to on the Tussock?"

"Quite right, sir." Mallett jumped from the car with a nimbleness Pettigrew could only envy, and opened the door for Eleanor to alight. "If you don't mind a bit of a scramble," he said, "I think the place for us is up *there.*"

He waved his arm to where, a short distance ahead and above, the smooth sweep of the hillside against the sky was broken by an outcrop of granite rocks. Pettigrew and Eleanor set off with him in their direction, but they had not gone far before, with a muttered excuse, Mallett turned back to the car. Halfway to their objective he overtook them again, tenderly bearing the picnic basket in his arms.

"Might want to be here for a little time," he explained. "No reason why we should starve."

A solitary blackcock flew off as they came near the rocks. Apart from him, they had the place to themselves. Following Mallett's lead they approached the rocks, keeping them between themselves and the skyline. The outcrop was in the form of a rough semicircle, and once within the perimeter it was possible to sit or lie in comfort and peer over its edge down the steep hillside on to the flat saddle below. Immediately beneath them ran the road, snaking across the Tussock before plunging down into the valley beyond. Midway along the road, perhaps two hundred yards away, a car was drawn up close into the side. Just beyond the car, on the opposite side of the road, was a small group of men. Pettigrew could distinguish the blue uniforms of two of them. One man seemed to be in a khaki shirt and shorts, the others in what are so quaintly called "lounge suits". They were looking at something on the ground.

Mallett dropped back from the rock on which he was lying to where he had deposited the basket, which he proceeded to open. From it he took a small leather case, and from the case a telescope. For some time he studied the group through the glass without speaking, then he handed it to Pettigrew. Pettigrew was not accustomed to a telescope. It took him some time to focus the instrument and even when he had done so, he found it almost impossible to keep it steady. But at last he conquered its difficulties, and the figures in the field of vision shewed up clearly and far larger than he had expected. When he had done, he proffered the glass to Eleanor, but she shook her head.

"I can't work a thing like that," she said. "Tell me."

Still Pettigrew said nothing. He was rather pale, she noticed, and he had wrinkled up his nose in a way that always meant that he was puzzled or unhappy.

"All right, then," said Eleanor softly. "Shall I tell you? The text you thought of just now. It was: *Where the carcase is, there shall the eagles be gathered together.*"

"Yes."

"And that's what happened—literally?"

"Not quite. The eagles are only metaphorical, unfortunately. But the carcase is literal."

"Well, it's all very interesting, but it can't be the one you saw on Saturday."

"That's what you'd think, isn't it?" said Pettigrew.

In the brief silence that followed, they saw the motor bicycle that had been approaching from Whitsea come to a standstill beside the police car. It did not stay there long. The uniformed constable, evidently posted there for the purpose, waved it on, and the rider went on his way, looking dangerously back over his shoulder as he did so. Then came the coach, to be dealt with in the same fashion.

"There'll be a lot more eagles about in a minute, I'm thinking," said Mallett. "There'll be photographers and an ambulance and men to take casts of footprints.

The Gathering of the Eagles

They'll block the view as best they can with police cars until they've got enough hurdles and screens to keep the place private. By that time there'll be a queue of cars and buses right across the Tussock, trying to stop and being moved on, and trying to move on and being stopped. It's wonderful how even an out of the way place like this fills up when there's a corpse involved. We only got here just in time to see anything."

"And what exactly have we seen?" said Eleanor.

There was an awkward little pause, and then Mallett said, "Well, Mr. Pettigrew, as your good lady said just now, it can't have been what you saw when you were having your little trip on horseback."

"It was exactly the same," said Pettigrew flatly.

"You told me he had on a bluey-grey coat, I remember. This one's green."

"I was wrong, that's all. I told you at the time my recollection was very vague. Now I've seen it again, I'm quite positive it's the one I saw before."

"Well then, sir, it is the same man, and he's been lying there ever since Saturday. You made a mistake about the place when you went back, that's all."

"I didn't make a mistake," said Pettigrew stubbornly. "He's in the same spot now that he was in when I first saw him—the place I went back to with Percy Percy when he wasn't there. You can mark it by those boulders. They're the only ones anywhere near the place."

"Well, then . . ." said Eleanor, and stopped abruptly. "Mr. Mallett," she went on, with a hint of desperation in her voice, "what do you really think?"

94

The Gathering of the Eagles

"I think," Mallett replied, "that we should all be the better for a little snack, madam."

The snack, as Pettigrew had expected, turned out to be a gargantuan meal. Such time as they were able to spare from the food that was continually pressed on them they devoted to contemplating the proceedings on the Tussock below, which followed very much the pattern that Mallett had foretold. He, meanwhile, kept up a running commentary on the spectacle, blending appreciation with criticism as the procedure of police investigation took its course. The meal and its accompaniment came to an end at about the same time. In the circle of rocks, the full fed guests made their final refusals of another helping, and brushed the last crumbs from their clothes. On the moor, the corpse, having been photographed from all angles, had been removed to the mortuary, and behind their screens junior policemen were settling down to a routine search of the surrounding ground. There was nothing more to see and nothing more that they were able to eat. It was peaceful among the rocks—peaceful, and decidedly warm. For the second time since his holiday began Pettigrew began to doze after a picnic meal. And once more, it was his wife's voice that jerked him awake.

"Have you considered precognition, Frank?"

"Considered—what?"

"Precognition. It's a possibility, you know."

Pettigrew reluctantly forced himself to consider it.

"You mean," he said, "that I might have seen what wasn't there at the time but was going to be there later?"

The Gathering of the Eagles

"Yes. Like the man who wrote *An Experiment with Time*."

"I don't think I'm a bit like the man who wrote *An Experiment with Time*. Things like that don't happen to me. I'm simply a normal bloke, with normal senses."

"Perhaps. But you weren't in an altogether normal state on Saturday afternoon. You were thinking about something you had seen on Bolter's Tussock fifty years ago—something that had made a tremendous impression on you at the time. You found yourself more or less reliving that experience. Subconsciously—if that's the right word—you were expecting to see it again. Nobody could have been surprised if you had seen it—or fancied that you had seen it, which is exactly the same thing. And all unknown to you, only just round the corner in time, something just like it was there, waiting to be seen. You took a jump forward three days, instead of backwards fifty years, and saw that instead. It seems a possible theory to me. Doesn't it to you?"

There are those who boast that they have second sight. There are even said to be families—mostly on the western fringes of the British Isles—in which any individual lacking it is regarded as eccentric. To Pettigrew, the idea that he might even for the space of a single afternoon, have been visited with the gift was utterly repellent. It was quite inconsistent with the character of logical formality that he had built up in a lifetime of hard work. The knowledge that deep down within him lurked a strong vein of fantasy made

96

him all the more anxious to disclaim the possibility.
But even as he opened his mouth to blast his wife's
ridiculous theory, the devil tempted him and he saw its
manifest attractions. It was neat, it was comprehensive,
above all it absolved him once and for all from the
duty of taking any action. He had only to concede that
for once in his life he had been "fey" and . . .

He found himself looking at Mallett.

"What is your opinion?" he asked.

Mallett was engaged in strapping up the picnic
basket. He pulled hard at a recalcitrant strap, and the
effort made his face rather red.

"You'll excuse me, sir," he said, "if I prefer not to
have any opinion on that subject. It's not in my line
at all. I've never see anything before it happened. It
would have saved me a lot of trouble if I had sometimes,
I dare say. But I can guess what's coming as well as
the next man, and if that's what precognition is,
then I precognose that we shall find things rather
badly upset when we get back to Sallowcombe."

"Why is that?"

"Has it occurred to you, sir, that in all the questions
we've been asking about the poor devil they've just
taken away in the ambulance, we never thought to
ask who he was? Well, it's difficult to be certain at this
range, but I had a good look at him through the glass,
and it's my belief that he's none other than Jack
Gorman."

97

CHAPTER X

Sunbeam Cottage

"I'm afraid it's not very much to look at," Mallett said apologetically as he stopped the car outside his house.

Pettigrew said nothing but privately he disagreed heartily. Sunbeam Cottage—such was its regrettable name—was a lot to look at—one might say, a great deal too much. In a country of soft colours and smooth curves it stood out, vivid, angular and irredeemably ugly. Happily the distressing exterior was redeemed by a cheerful, comfortable interior. Mallett insisted on taking them all over it while the kettle boiled for tea. Back in the sitting-room he said:

"Well, now, Mrs. Pettigrew, what do you think of it?"

Eleanor murmured something that she hoped would satisfy an obviously house-proud owner, but Mallett brushed it aside.

"I'm speaking of the spare room, of course," he said. "It's not so large as the one at Sallowcombe, but do you think it will do?"

"Do? For what?"

"For you and Mr. Pettigrew. Unless, of course, you've given up the idea of an Exmoor holiday altogether. You'll hardly get in anywhere else at this time of year."

98

"But why——?" Eleanor began. "Oh, I see. You're assuming that Mrs. Gorman is—will be——"

"I'm assuming that Mrs. Gorman is now a widow, that she'll be too upset to be wanting to bother with boarders and that in any case you won't care to stay in a house with that sort of trouble about. And I've gone so far as to assume that you and Mr. Pettigrew might care to stay with me for a few days. I'm sorry to be so blunt about it, but as I told Mr. Pettigrew yesterday, I've lost my finesse living in the country."

"It's extremely kind of you, Mr. Mallett."

"You'll come, then? Good! As my guests, mind. I don't want any nonsense about paying your way. You can leave a present for the housekeeper at the end of your stay, but that's as far as I'll go."

Mallett accompanied his words with a ferocious tug at the ends of his moustache. Thoroughly overawed, the Pettigrews agreed to his proposition, provided that his basic assumption proved to be correct.

It was correct. Mr. Joliffe's little car was standing in the farmyard when they returned to Sallowcombe, and it was Mr. Joliffe who received them when they entered.

"My daughter is in bed," he said heavily. "She has had some news that has upset her. I was sent for from Whitsea."

"We have heard the news," said Pettigrew. "I should like to express our deep sympathy."

"That's very good of you, sir, but frankly I don't regard it as an occasion for sympathy at all. Rationally speaking, it's a very happy release for her. My daughter, however, isn't rational. She doesn't see it in that light at all. She has not so much as set eyes on her husband for six months, and now she chooses to be prostrated. Women are strange creatures, if you'll excuse the phrase, Mrs. Pettigrew."

From the look on his wife's face, Francis Pettigrew realized that she was not disposed to excuse the phrase and that for two pins she would make the fact extremely clear. He interposed hastily.

"In any case, Mr. Joliffe, I am sure that you will agree that at a moment like this your daughter won't want any visitors in the house. We have been lucky enough to find somewhere to go, so we shall be leaving straight away."

"I was afraid you would say that. I told my daughter as much, but she didn't pay any attention. I'll get out your bill while you do your packing." He sighed deeply. "In the ordinary way I should charge you for a week's board in lieu of notice, but in the circumstances I can hardly do that. It's a pity, but there it is."

Pettigrew contrived to keep a straight face. "I'm sorry," he murmured.

"Ah well," Mr. Joliffe went on, "there's one good thing about it. The next lot of boarders aren't due till Saturday week and she should be over it by then. I shouldn't like to put them off—that sort of thing gives the house a bad name."

"Disgusting old man!" Eleanor burst out as soon as they were back in their room. "Heartless, money-grubbing brute! And I thought he was *nice*!"

Sunbeam Cottage

"I'm disappointed in him too," said Pettigrew.
He was looking out of the window as he spoke, and his
gaze rested on the roof of the outhouse beneath Mrs.
Gorman's room. Remembering what he had seen
there a few nights before, he felt it unreasonable that
she should be so overcome with grief at her husband's
death. To that extent at least he could sympathize with
Mr. Joliffe.

"Those poor little girls!" Eleanor went on. "He
hadn't a word of sympathy for them, of course. I
really wonder whether we are doing right in leaving
until we're sure Mrs. Gorman is in a fit state to look
after them. I feel quite worried about them."

That worry at least was dispelled when, the packing
completed, Pettigrew sought out Mr. Joliffe to settle his
account. He found him closeted with his granddaughters, and it was obvious at a glance that a condition
of complete sympathy existed between them. Beryl was
sitting in the corner absorbing a sweet of the type known
to Pettigrew in his youth as a gob-stopper. Though her
face bore traces of recent tears, she looked resigned,
and even contented. Doreen was close to her grand-
father's side, and it was evident that Pettigrew had
interrupted an intimate colloquy between them. Her
expression was subdued and serious, and for the first
time Pettigrew was aware of her strong resemblance to
her mother. But what struck him most was the look of
utter confidence on one side and deep affection on the
other.

In a gentler voice than usual, Joliffe told the two
girls to "run along" while he did his business with the

departing guest. "They're all I have, Mr. Pettigrew," he said softly as the door closed behind them. The sentimental expression vanished from his face as he went on, almost without pause, "Was it one or two early morning teas you had on Saturday?"

Pettigrew paid his bill. Mr. Joliffe shook him warmly by the hand and expressed the hope that they would meet again another year. "The rooms will be there," he said, "and if Mrs. Gorman is there to look after you, you'll be welcome. It just doesn't pay if you have to give a woman wages to attend to the summer visitors. My daughter was talking of setting up house on her own, but now this has happened I am hoping she will change her mind."

Pettigrew must have shown something of what he felt, for Joliffe went on, "You think I'm lacking in sympathy for my daughter, sir, but if you'd known my son-in-law you'd think different. He was a ne'er-do-well, and that's the long and the short of it. I don't mind telling you that first to last he cost me a lot of money. Thank Heaven, he's left my girl well provided for!"

After this, Pettigrew could not resist the temptation of adding to Mr. Joliffe's financial worries by demanding a twopenny stamp on his receipt.

Mallett was out when the Pettigrews returned to Sunbeam Cottage and he did not put in an appearance until just before supper.

"I've been having a chat with the Detective Inspector," he said. "Luckily we're on fairly good terms."

He filled three glasses with sherry and handed them round. "Inquest's on Thursday, it seems. At Polton. Your very good healths, sir and madam."

The sherry was of a quality to command Pettigrew's respect, but for the moment his mind was on lower things.

"What else did he tell you?" he asked.

"I didn't like to ask any direct questions, because he's a sensitive sort of man, and might have resented them, coming from me. But I gathered that death was due to a blow in the chest. The Inspector seems to be working on the theory that it was a motor car, but it might have been something else, so far as he can tell until he gets the report of the P.M."

"But he wasn't found on the road," Eleanor put in.

"Quite so, ma'am. It seems the body had been moved after death."

"And death was—when?"

"It was the answer to that question that I was angling for all along, of course, but it took me a long time to bring him round to it. And the answer—again without waiting for the pathologist's report—appears to be, late last night or first thing this morning."

Mallett looked at Eleanor. Eleanor looked at Frank. Frank looked at his glass. Nobody said anything for a moment.

"So that lets you out, Mr. Pettigrew," said Mallett cheerfully.

"Yes. That lets me out, doesn't it? I'm simply a second-sighted, temperamental sufferer from precognition. It's nice to know. It only remains to enjoy the rest of the holiday." He drank off his glass with a singular absence of enjoyment.

The appearance of supper restored Pettigrew's spirits, and by the end of the evening he was able to discuss the case of Jack Gorman—for it was impossible to keep away from it for long—in his usual vein of cheerful detachment.

"I must go to the inquest," he said. "Usually they are dull affairs, though the last one I attended turned out to be unexpectedly exciting. But one wants to know something of the background to appreciate them properly. There's an odd background to this case, obviously. I'd like to know why he wasn't living with his wife and family, to begin with."

"I can answer that one," said Mallett. "The Gorman family row made quite a noise in the neighbourhood last year. Everyone expected Joliffe to prosecute, but he was persuaded not to in the end."

"I have it on Mr. Joliffe's authority that his son-in-law was a ne'er-do-well, who cost him a lot of money. Was the projected prosecution for embezzlement, by any chance?"

"Yes. I'd better tell the story from the beginning, so far as I know it. The Gormans are a well-known family in these parts, and Jack Gorman was the best known of the lot when he was a bachelor. He was very good-looking for one thing, a first-rate horseman and a good shot—a wonderful dancer, I believe. It's not surprising he attracted Edna Joliffe."

"What is surprising to me is that her father ever allowed her to marry him."

Sunbeam Cottage

"She married without his consent. He wouldn't speak to her for years. She is a very determined little woman, in her quiet way, you know. She needed a lot of determination to stick to Jack, as it turned out. He was a rolling stone, though his travels didn't take him further south than Exeter or further east than Bristol. He tried a lot of things—a bit of farming, a good deal of horse-coping, keeping a seaside hotel. He lost money at all of them, and at his last job he lost his licence into the bargain. Finally his father-in-law took pity on him —or rather on his own daughter and grandchildren. He took him and the family into Sallowcombe, and found Jack a job in the butchery business at Whitsea, with the prospect of a partnership if he made the grade."

"What made him change his mind like that? It seems out of character."

"I've only gossip to go on for this, but I fancy it's reliable. You may have noticed that Joliffe is not exactly uninterested in money. Well about this time the rumour began to go round that Jack had pretty substantial expectations under the will of some aged Gorman or another. I told you there was supposed to be money in the family somewhere, you may remember."

"I think I know where. But go on."

"Joliffe was prepared to forgive a good deal in a son-in-law with expectations, and it was a wonderful chance for Jack, if he could have kept straight. But you might as well have tried to straighten a corkscrew. The job lasted just a year, and at the end of that time old Joliffe had his accounts specially audited. That was the end of Master Jack's career in the butchery trade. It was the end of his marriage too, to all intents. For when he went, Edna decided to stay with her father, and I for one don't blame her."

"She didn't mean to stay any longer than she had to," said Pettigrew. "She was going back to her husband as soon as he came into his money."

"I don't know where you got that from, sir. But even if it's true, she might have had to wait a very long time."

"I got it from two unimpeachable sources—first from the two little girls and then from Mr. Joliffe himself. As for the money, that's just the irony of it—Jack Gorman came into his inheritance last Sunday."

"Did he now?" said Mallett. "That seems a remarkably convenient arrangement."

CHAPTER XI

Inquest

Next day the weather broke. Pettigrew looked out of his bedroom window on to a wide, watery landscape. The moors that had bounded his view the day before had disappeared in mist, and across the middle distance the rain was being driven in almost horizontal lines by the violent west wind. It was the kind of scene that was part and parcel of his Exmoor memories. Up to that moment there had been something lacking in the evocation of the past, and now he realized what it was. The continued fine weather had been against the order of nature. This was the real thing.

"I shall go for a walk this morning," he announced at breakfast, and nothing that Eleanor could say could stop him. He ridiculed the idea of catching cold. The wind, though strong, was from the west, and therefore warm. The air was soft and mild. Nobody ever took harm from merely getting wet. In any case he had a perfectly good mackintosh. Exercise was an essential if he was going to have any appetite for lunch. And so on.

What Pettigrew expected to get out of his walk he did not know. What in fact he got, as anybody could have told him he would, was a heavy cold. He disguised the fact as long as was humanly possible, but in the end it had to be accepted. For the second time in a week he was housebound, and this time it could not be suggested that it was anything but his own fault.

What made his position particularly annoying to Pettigrew was that he was unable to fulfil the promise he had made to himself of attending the inquest on Jack Gorman. Mallett therefore went unaccompanied. Although he was far too civil a man to hint such a thing Mallett was distinctly relieved to be alone on this occasion. Purely as an observer, he was genuinely interested in what he instinctively felt to be an unusual case. He had no theories about it, and went with an entirely open mind. The presence of a companion with an altogether fantastic theory would be merely up-setting. Reflecting on Pettigrew's story, Mallett shook his head sadly as he went out to his garage through the still pouring rain. He had the utmost respect for his old friend, but decidedly he was not the man he once had been.

The inquest was held in the long room behind the Staghunter's Arms, the room in which, in default of a village hall, most of the local meetings, celebrations and functions took place. It was already nearly full when Mallett arrived. There were a great many familiar faces, including almost all of the local branches of the Gorman clan. Not quite all, however. The widow of the deceased was absent. So was her father. On the other hand, there was present in the front row a stout lady in deep mourning who was unknown to Mallett. From her complacent manner and the air of gracious condescension with which from time to time she addressed the lesser Gormans around and behind her, it was clear that she was, in her own eyes at least, an important personage.

By the time fixed for the opening of the inquest the room was as full as it could hold. The air vibrated with the deep bass of West Country talk. The temperature rose steadily. A quarter of an hour later in a sudden silence the coroner entered and took his seat. He was a stranger to the gathering—almost a foreigner, in fact. It was credibly reported that he lived as far away as the other side of Taunton. That was one offence in the eyes of his audience. His unpunctuality was another. His failure to apologize for it was a third. Fortunately, perhaps, for him, the coroner was unconscious of the waves of disapproval projected at him from the body of the hall. He was a small, spare man with the beak and eye of a farmyard fowl and a fowl's trick of dipping his head from time to time as though to peck up some grain of information.

A jury was sworn in and the coroner without further preamble observed, "I shall first call evidence of identification. Louisa Gorman, will you come into the box?"

The stout lady in black rose with massive dignity. She contrived to give the air of walking in procession as she covered the short distance to the improvised witness box. It was clear that this was her big moment and that she meant to make the most of it. She gave her address as Tracy Grange, Minster Tracy.

"And have you this morning seen the body of a man

and do you identify that body as that of John Richard Gorman?"

"That was him all right."

The coroner noted her answer, and for an instant it seemed that Louisa's big moment was going to be over almost before it had began. But then the coroner took a peck at his desk, fixed her with his beady eye and asked,

"Let me see, madam, what relation were you to the deceased? Were you his sister?"

"Sister? Of course not! Do I look like his sister?" Louisa appealed with a knowing look to her audience of Gormans, and she and they joined together in open derision at the outsider's ignorance.

"Very well, madam. There is no occasion for incivility. What relation were you?"

"We were cousins, if you want to know."

"And he lived with you at Minster Tracy?"

"He certainly did not." Louisa tossed her head·in scorn. "I live at the big house at Minster. He lived in a caravan on our land."

"By himself?"

"That's right. He'd been on his own since his wife threw him out."

"You let him put his caravan there?"

"I didn't—'twasn't my land. Gilbert did—my brother."

"And when did you last see the deceased?"

"Who, Jack? That would be Friday afternoon."

"Last Friday? You have not seen him since?"

Louisa reflected.

Inquest

"It was two days before Gilbert was took," she said. "And that was Sunday. Yes, it was Friday I saw him."

"How came he to see you on that day?"

"He came on his flat feet. He used to have a motor bike, but the hire-purchase took it back."

"I mean—why did he come to see you?"

"It was my brother Gilbert he came to see, and he came to borrow money. That was all he ever came for. He had some story about being behind with his payments to the Court for that girl's baby, but it's my belief he wanted it for a horse to go out with the hounds from Satcherly Way on Saturday. I told him Gilbert was ill, but he would see him. After all, blood's thicker'n water, and Jack was going to get Tracy when Gilbert died. It's that makes everything so awkward now."

The coroner looked hopelessly out of his depth.

"I don't think I need go into all that now," he said. "You had no occasion to see him since?"

"I had occasion all right, when Gilbert was took so ill on Sunday. I sent for him then, but the caravan was empty and the bed not slept in."

"And that surprised you?"

Louisa shrugged her shoulders.

A voice from the back of the hall broke in on the colloquy between coroner and witness.

"There was lots of beds Jack liked a heap better'n his own," it said.

The audience roared its appreciation of the simple joke. Only Louisa and the coroner, for once united, disapproved.

Inquest

"That's quite enough from you, Jim Cantle,"
shouted Louisa. "When I get you outside, I'll——

The coroner rapped his desk. "If there is any further
disturbance I shall clear the court," he said. "Are there
any questions you want to ask this witness, members
of the jury?" Without waiting for their reply, he went
on rapidly, "No? Thank you, madam, you may stand
down. Call the next witness, please. John Mainprice."

John Mainprice proved to be an embarrassed young
hiker who had stumbled on Jack Gorman's body on
Tuesday morning just off the road across Bolter's
Tussock. He was soon disposed of, and the coroner
passed on to the medical evidence.

Medicine, like law, has an esoteric vocabulary of its
own, not to be comprehended by the vulgar. Medical
men at least can, if they choose, put their opinions into
perfectly intelligible language. This particular medical
man—a cocksure young fellow with an aggravating air
of omniscience—did not so choose. His evidence was
couched in a technical jargon which delighted the
coroner—who himself had medical qualifications—and
mystified his hearers. Mallett, with the experience of
countless homicidal enquiries behind him, was able
to follow well enough. Jack Gorman had died from
shock following multiple injuries. Of these injuries the
gravest were concentrated in one area of the body.
Three broken ribs—extensive bruising—gross injury
to the internal organs, all described with loving ana-
tomical particularity by the witness. The minor injuries could have been caused by falling on a hard
surface, or, he added as an afterthought, being run

over by the vehicle that had knocked him down. No, he did not state as a fact that the deceased had been knocked down by a motor vehicle. Any other moving object sufficiently hard and weighty could have had the same effect. Personally, he could not think of one offhand likely to be met with at this particular place. The injuries were *consistent* with being knocked down by a motor vehicle—perhaps that was the fairer way to put it. Death had occurred in the early hours of Tuesday morning or late on Monday night. He gathered up his papers and withdrew, exuding self-satisfaction from every pore.

The evidence of Detective Inspector Parkinson wound up the proceedings. Like that of the last witness it was technical, but it was easy enough to understand. He described in careful detail the position of the body, illustrating what he said from photographs. He had found it at a spot in the heather some three yards distant from the road itself, but less than a yard from the nearest point to which a motor car could drive. In fact, tracks shewed clearly that a number of vehicles had pulled off the road at this place, one of the few level strips of roadside on the Tussock. It was a favourite spot for picnickers. Indeed, he had found beneath the body the remains of a picnic meal, wrapped in a portion of a Sunday newspaper—last Sunday's newspaper, he added significantly. There were clear indications that the deceased had been placed in the position where he was found after death, or, at all events, after the injuries had been inflicted. Further enquiries were proceeding on the assumption that this had been done by the driver of the motor vehicle concerned. Traffic over the Tussock was particularly heavy at holiday periods, and there were a great many more investigations to be made. He respectfully asked the coroner for an adjournment *sine die.*

And on this inconclusive note the proceedings proper ended. To the great delight of the assembled company, however, they were succeeded by what might be fairly called proceedings improper.

A stalwart young man with a round red face arose from the middle of the hall, and said, "Mr. Coroner! Is that there all the evidence we're going to have?"

The coroner pecked at him sharply.

"That is all the evidence that will be called to-day. You heard what the police officer said; there are further enquiries to be made."

"Will he be enquiring where Jack was Saturday and Sunday?"

"If you have any information, Mr.——"

"Gorman, the name is. Richard Gorman, Beechanger Farm. They call me Dick."

"If you have any information, have a talk to the Inspector, and tell him anything you know about this matter. Now, members of the jury——"

"It's not for me to tell him anything. I don't know anything. But I know a fiddle when I see one, and that's what there's been yere—a fair fiddle!"

He stalked from the room. In the momentary confusion that followed, Mallett noticed Tom Gorman, who had been sitting just behind Louisa, get up and follow him. He waited, himself, until the proceedings had been formally adjourned and then went out with the rest into the soft, damp Exmoor afternoon.

Pushing his way through the crowd, Mallett avoided various acquaintances who shewed signs of wishing to speak to him. He wanted rather badly to be alone, to think over what he had seen and heard. But he was to be disappointed. As he turned into the Inn yard where he had left his car, he almost walked into Tom and Dick Gorman, deep in conversation. At the sight of him, Dick turned, and edging him into the wall, fairly forced him to a standstill.

"Ah!" said Dick. "Just the man we want, isn't he, Tom?"

Tom said nothing, but he stood with his arms akimbo in a position to cut off Mallett's retreat. He was a large man—not so large as Mallett by a good way, but at least thirty years younger. Dick was smaller, but compact and muscular. Mallett did not want a rough house, in any event. He said mildly,

"What can I do for you?"

"There's a man who said he saw Jack on the Tussock on Saturday—I hear he's staying with you," said Dick truculently. "What's his name, Tom?"

"Betty something," said Tom. "Funny name for a man, but that's what it sounded like."

"I have some visitors," said Mallett cautiously. "A Mr. and Mrs. Pettigrew."

"What I want to know is," Dick persisted, "did he see Jack or not?"

"It's no use asking me that," said Mallett firmly. "In any case," he turned to Tom, "you should know the

115

answer as well as I do. You were with him on Saturday, I understand. If your brother——"

"Not my brother," said Tom. "Second cousin, isn't it, Dick?"

"That's right. And brother-in-law. I married his sister and he married mine."

Mallett sighed. He had long since ceased trying to chart the ramifications of the Gorman clan.

"If he really believes it, why doesn't he talk to the Inspector, as the coroner said?"

"It's Tom ought to talk to the Inspector, not me," Dick broke in. "He was there."

"I didn't see anything," said Tom. "There wasn't anything to see. Mr. Olding will tell you that."

"But you don't believe Jack was killed on Monday night, do you?" Dick's voice had an urgency of appeal in it that astonished Mallett.

"I don't understand," he said. "Even supposing it did turn out that Jack Gorman died on Saturday instead of Monday, what earthly difference is that going to make to either of you?"

There was no answer to his question, but the silence that succeeded it seemed charged with meaning. Tom looked at Dick and Dick at Tom and the expression on their faces told Mallett that he had stumbled on the meaning of the whole strange little episode.

"It might make a difference and it mightn't." Tom's voice was quiet and reflective. "From what Mr. Bulford says, it seems that it might. That's just the point."

"And who may Mr. Bulford be?"

"He's the lawyer up to Wiveliscombe. Would you like to go to Wiveliscombe to-morrow and have a word with him? I could run you up in my car—it won't cost you a penny."

"Why on earth should I want to talk to your lawyer —or he to me?"

"Now look here, Mr. Mallett," said Dick persuasively. "You heard what I told that fool of a coroner just now. There's been a fiddle over this business—or looks like there has. And if so, there's enquiries to be made—that's what Mr. Bulford says. You can forget about your Betty friend—he don't count. There's someone else behind all this and we want to know who. And we reckon you're the chap to find out. It's your sort of work, isn't it? There's fifty pounds in it for you, all for asking a few questions. Now, what do you say?"

Mallett was tugging at his moustache ends until it felt that the hair must come out at the roots—a sign, in him, of intense emotion. Had he but known it, his sensations at that moment were very much the same as those experienced by Pettigrew a few days before, at the sound of the hunting horn. Only in his case the memories evoked were far more recent, and for that reason more compelling. He could think of a dozen reasons why he should turn a deaf ear to the offer, but . . .

"I don't mind going to Wiveliscombe with you to-morrow," he said. "Mind you, I make no promises— none whatever. Is that understood?"

"That's understood, all right, Mr. Mallett."

"One other thing, before we go any further. If I

117

should undertake this enquiry, and if anything should come of it, it will be no use asking me to stop half-way. I shall find out all I can. And if what I find out seems likely to disclose a criminal offence, then I go straight to the police, *no matter who the criminal may turn out to be,* and it will be too late to ask me to hush it up. Is that also understood?"

For the life of him, Mallett could not have said why he spoke with so much vehemence, especially as he had not even decided to accept the commission which had been offered him in such vague terms. But there was a streak of melodrama in him, and to his own ears, at least, it sounded most impressive. One at least of his hearers was impressed. Dick's face was solemn as he answered, "Yes, sir, I accept that."

Tom was not quite so ready with his reply, and there was a gleam of what could have been amusement in his heavy face as he said, "Surely, Mr. Mallett, surely. We'll call for you to-morrow about ten, then?"

CHAPTER XII

The Price of a Ham

"I really believe," said Pettigrew, "that spring has begun at last."

"You said that," Eleanor reminded him, "two weeks ago."

"Now you mention it, I believe I did. It was the usual false alarm. I should have known better. But this is the real thing. There's a softness in the air that's quite unmistakable. *Winter's rains and ruins are over, and all the season——*"

"Please, Frank! Not at breakfast!"

"I apologize. Swinburne at breakfast should be left to undergraduates. I will moderate my transports by looking at my post. It should have a thoroughly deadening effect—nothing but bills and circulars, by the look of it."

He slit open one envelope after another with a resigned expression. Near the bottom of the pile he found something that was neither bill nor circular.

Pettigrew read the letter through in silence. Then he laid it down beside his plate, and sat for a while, looking at nothing in particular, drumming his fingers on the table, wrinkling his nose as was his habit in moods of anxiety or doubt.

The Price of a Ham

"If you're not going to eat any breakfast," said Eleanor, reproachfully, "I am. Won't you cut a slice of ham, or shall I do it myself?"

Pettigrew came out of his abstraction with a jerk.

"No woman is to be trusted with a ham," he declared. "Particularly a superb specimen like this. Let me do it."

He went across to the sideboard, carved two slices from the fine ham that was there, and stood back to admire his handiwork. Then he began to laugh quietly. He was still laughing when he returned to the table.

"Is this a private joke?" Eleanor asked, her mouth full of ham. "Or can anyone join in ?"

"It has only just dawned on me. Didn't Mallett send us this ham last week?"

"You know perfectly well he did. It's twice the size of anything I should have wanted to buy, even if I could afford it."

"And why, do you think, should he take it into his head to do such a thing, just at this moment?"

"It was simply a kind thought, I suppose."

"There was no letter with it, was there?"

"Just a card with his name on it and some polite message," said Eleanor. "You saw it yourself. But Frank, why——"

"It's the first message of any sort we've had from him since we left Exmoor," Pettigrew persisted. "He's not sent us so much as a line all that time. Even Mr. Joliffe was good for a threepenny Christmas card, but Mallett was mum. I particularly asked him to let me know what happened about the Gorman inquest, but he never did a thing about it. Why is that, do you imagine?"

"Frank, dear," said Eleanor gently. "Don't be cross with me, but I'm afraid that is my fault. You see, you have been sleeping so much better ever since we came home, and I didn't want you upset. I asked Mr. Mallett not to write."

"I see. That makes it funnier than ever. He's not allowed to write, so he says it with hams."

"But, Frank, I do assure you, there's been nothing for him to write about. Since the inquest was adjourned all those months ago, nothing whatever has happened. The police have made all sorts of enquiries, of course, and the whole neighbourhood was full of rumours for a time, but nobody was ever arrested over poor Jack Gorman's death, and little by little the whole thing has died down."

"You seem to be remarkably well up in the matter," said Pettigrew. "How is that?"

"Well, as I'd told Mr. Mallett that he wasn't to bother you with letters, I thought I had better keep an eye on things," Eleanor explained. "So I asked Hester Greenway to keep me informed. She has really been very helpful. I hope you don't mind. I wanted to save you being worried."

"That was a kind thought of yours. But as it happened, I was anxious not to worry you. You needn't have troubled Hester. I've discovered a man at Mark-hampton who comes from Exmoor and takes in the local paper regularly. Every week I've been through it from cover to cover to see if there was any hint of developments in the affair. And there has been none."

"Well, then. . . ." said Eleanor. "There's nothing for either of us to worry about, is there? Or—or is there?"

By way of reply, Pettigrew tossed across the table the letter that he had been reading. It bore at the top an imposingly long list of names and an address in Lincoln's Inn. It ran:

"Dear Sir,

  Re Gorman, decd; Gorman v. Southern Bank Ltd. and Another.

We are acting as London agents for Messrs. Bulford and Langrish of Wiveliscombe on behalf of the Plaintiff in the above matter. It is an action shortly to be heard in the Chancery Division of the High Court of Justice in which the Plaintiff claims (inter alia) a declaration that John Richard Gorman, deceased, predeceased Gilbert Amos Gorman, deceased. We are given to understand that you may be in a position to assist the Plaintiff. We should accordingly esteem it a favour if you would attend at our office at a date convenient to yourself in the near future when our Mr. Fitzgibbon could take a proof of evidence from you.

We would add that this letter is written on the advice of Mr. Manktelow of counsel (who is, we believe, personally known to you) and that he has further advised us to secure your attendance, if necessary, by *sub poena ad testificandum.* We trust, however, that you will not oblige us to resort to this expedient.

The Price of a Ham

With apologies for troubling you in this matter, we remain,

Your obedient servants,
Harkness, Fitzgibbon, Blandy & Co."

Eleanor read the letter through twice before handing it back.

"I don't see what this has got to do with the Southern Bank," she remarked.

"Oh, they're only in the action because they're trustees or executors of a will, or something like that. I'm not worrying about *them*."

"Then all this nonsense about deceased and predeceased. I don't understand it."

"I understand only too well. Gilbert Gorman died on —I forget the date, but it was a Sunday—the day I was laid up in bed at Sallowcombe. At least—obviously one must be careful in these matters—that was the day the news of his death came to Sallowcombe. But from what I overheard on the telephone, I think we can assume he did die on that Sunday."

"And Jack died on Monday night or Tuesday morning. That's what the coroner said. Isn't that final?"

"Obviously it isn't, as someone is trying to get the Chancery Court to say something different."

"Why should they?"

"There could be quite a number of reasons for that. Suppose Jack was Gilbert's next of kin, for instance. . . . No, it can't be quite as simple as that. But does it matter? The point is, someone is trying to prove that Jack died first."

The Price of a Ham

"But I thought we'd decided that he didn't. I mean . . ."

There was an embarrassed pause before Pettigrew spoke again.

"Has it occurred to you," he said, "what sort of a figure I should cut in the witness-box, explaining to a Chancery judge that I had been indulging in—what did you call it?—precognition?"

"But if that's what you had been doing——"

Pettigrew put his coffee cup down with a clatter.

"I've been quietening my conscience all this time by telling myself that it didn't matter," he said. "Jack's body turned up in due course and the coroner sat on him and no harm was done. Now it seems that it does matter, and harm may have been done. It's a judgment on me for shirking my plain duty as a citizen and trying to hide behind a lot of psychological mumbo-jumbo. I'm going to be made to look ridiculous, and serve me right."

"But, Frank, is anybody going to believe your story against all the other evidence? Surely it's much more likely that you should have been mistaken than everyone else?"

"If my evidence stood alone, this case would never have been brought. Obviously, it doesn't. That's where Mallett's ham comes in. He's the man responsible for the whole business, and the ham was his way of apologizing for landing me in this mess."

"Really, Frank! You're imagining things."

"I'm certainly not. I'm beginning to remember them, though. The day after the inquest, Mallett said he had to go to Wiveliscombe. He didn't go in his own car. Someone called for him. The next day he was out all day. I thought at the time that he was sheepish and silent about where he'd been and what he was doing. It's perfectly obvious. He was the only available person with the knowledge and the intelligence to ferret this matter out. Someone took him to see these solicitors at Wiveliscombe and from then on he was employed by them to cook up this case. He must have felt rather uncomfortable having us in the house all the time."

"I thought he seemed quite relieved when we went," Eleanor remarked. "That would explain it. But that was nearly six months ago. Why has it taken all this time to bring it to court?"

"All this time? Good heavens, woman, this is a Chancery suit. It's the nearest thing to greased lightning in my experience. What I can't make out is how it has got to this stage so quickly."

CHAPTER XIII

Re Gorman, Deceased

To a layman, there is probably little to choose between the various courts of law that are to be found in the vast Gothic pile at the eastern end of the Strand. They vary somewhat in size, but, large or small, they are alike in their dingy livery of grey stone and fumed oak, in their austerely uncomfortable furnishings, in their lancet windows, ingeniously designed to exclude any stray shaft of light that might wander into this quarter of London. To the connoisseur, however, distinctions, invisible to the outsider, leap to the eye. To him, the difference between a Court of Queen's Bench and one of Chancery is as obvious and as pronounced as the difference between Oxford and Cambridge.

Pettigrew was a common law man to the marrow of his bones, and when, a few weeks later, he pushed open the door of Chancery Court VI, he wished with all his heart that it was Queen's Bench Court IV just round the corner. The whole atmosphere was alien. The very usher's shoes squeaked equity. For all the superficial familiarity of his surroundings, he felt a stranger in a strange land.

At least, there were plenty of familiar faces in the

126

body of the court. Not without surprise, he saw Mrs. Gorman sitting in a corner near the back. Her quiet, patient face seemed in some way altered, but he could not determine in what the change consisted. He looked round for Mr. Joliffe, and found him in the opposite corner, at the furthest possible remove from his daughter that was consistent with sitting in the same row. They were ignoring one another's presence with an intensity possible only to close relations. Further forward, just behind counsel's seats, was Tom Gorman, stiff and uncomfortable in a new suit. Sitting with Tom was another, smaller man with a strong family likeness to him. He was whispering to a man with a bright-red west-country complexion whom Pettigrew took to be the solicitor from Wiveliscombe. Then Mallett appeared silently in the doorway and padded quietly down to take his seat behind Tom. Mallett seemed out of place in these surroundings. Still more so did the man who followed him—a plain-clothes policeman if ever Pettigrew saw one.

The stage seemed to be set. Pettigrew, waiting patiently for the curtain to go up, wondered what the play was to be about. He had forfeited the opportunity of finding out, because, from a mixture of motives which he had never brought himself to analyse, he had declined Mr. Fitzgibbon's pressing invitation to give him a proof of his evidence. He was attending obedient to his subpoena to testify in a cause the nature of which he could only guess. Even the parties were uncertain. The cause list stuck up in the corridor outside the court told him that the Plaintiff was Gorman, R. P., and the initials meant nothing to him. He derived a certain amusement from the situation.

Manktelow came in, talking to another counsel, evidently his opponent, whose face was unfamiliar to Pettigrew. While his clerk deposited on the desk in front of him a formidable brief and half a dozen volumes of Law Reports, he looked round the court and caught Pettigrew's eye. But before he could do more than smile his recognition, the door at the back of the bench was opened, and the court rose as Mr. Justice Pomeroy entered to take his seat.

"May it please your lordship," said Manktelow. "In this case I appear on behalf of the Plaintiff, Mr. Richard Petherick Gorman, who is a party interested in the settlement to which I shall have to refer your lordship in a moment. My learned friend Mr. Twentyman appears for the Southern Bank Ltd., who are the trustees of the settlement and the first Defendants in the action. The second Defendant, Mrs. Edna Mary Gorman"—he lowered his voice to break the shocking news—"she, my lord, is not represented. She has entered an appearance but taken no further part in the proceedings. She appears here in person."

"In person, Mr. Manktelow? In a case of this nature, that is very unusual."

"Unusual and unfortunate, my lord. I think I should tell your lordship that those instructing me have more than once urged Mrs. Gorman to take advice in the matter. So far as the costs were concerned my client was prepared to give an undertaking——"

Re Gorman, Deceased

"Is Mrs. Gorman present?"

"I am here, my lord."

Mrs. Gorman stood up, a not particularly good-looking woman, dressed in country-made black clothes, her low voice barely carrying across the court. Once more, Pettigrew was struck by a change in her appearance. He could not determine what it was, but for some reason or another she seemed a far more impressive personality now than he remembered her.

"I am here, my lord," she repeated.

"Mrs. Gorman, I understand——"

"As this gentleman says, I haven't got a lawyer," Mrs. Gorman went on as though the Judge had not spoken. And for some reason her calm insistence on saying her piece in complete disregard of the fact that he was addressing her did not seem to savour of disrespect. "I don't think I need a lawyer, seeing that all I want is for the truth to be known. I'm sure you'll help me over that, my lord. I only hope the truth won't hurt my children, but if it does it can't be helped."

She sat down again. There was an awkward little pause. Then the Judge cleared his throat and said, "Very well, Mr. Manktelow."

"As your lordship pleases. My lord, if I may come at once to the point of this action, it is to determine the order in which two of the persons named in the settlement died. One of them is Gilbert Amos Gorman, and he died, according to his Death Certificate which is before me, on Sunday, September the 10th. My lord, no question arises as to that death. It was a natural one—polycystic disease of the kidneys, I observe—and

129

nobody doubts that he did in fact expire on that date. The other person is John Richard Gorman, the husband of the second Defendant, and the cause of his death is described as shock and internal haemorrhage, the date being recorded in the Certificate as Tuesday, September the 12th. My lord, the contention of the Plaintiff is that that date is wrong. His case will be that John died on or before Saturday, September the 9th."

"You say that the Death Certificate is wrong, Mr. Manktelow?"

"My lord, I do, and in order that I may put the difficulties before me as clearly as possible, let me add that the Certificate was issued in accordance with the instructions of the coroner after an inquest with a jury. My task is to persuade your lordship that the coroner was wrong. I say that he was wrong, that the witnesses, lay and medical, called before him were wrong, that they were deliberately misled and deceived in the interests of the second Defendant and to the prejudice of my client, the Plaintiff."

The judicial eyebrows shot up. "You say that Mrs. Gorman did all that, Mr. Manktelow?"

"My lord, I do not. It is, of course, not necessary to my case to affix responsibility to anybody, provided I prove my contention, but incidentally I shall call evidence indicating who in my submission is responsible."

"Very well. Perhaps you will come to the settlement now?"

"If your lordship pleases. My lord, those instructing me have prepared a table shewing the pedigree of the various persons involved, and if your lordship has it beside you when the settlement is being read, it will perhaps be of some assistance."

Manktelow's instructing solicitors had not been niggardly in the matter of providing copies of the pedigree, and Pettigrew with a little manœuvring was able to obtain one. He was disappointed to find that it did not give in full what he knew to be the almost endless ramifications of the Gorman family but confined itself to those with whom the settlement was concerned. None the less he found it not without interest:

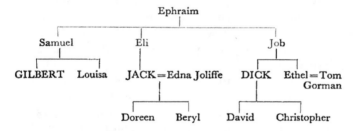

"In preparing the exhibit, my lord," Manktelow was saying, "I have ventured to substitute for the baptismal names of the characters the names by which they were habitually known, in order to avoid confusion. Thus John Richard Gorman is Jack and Richard Petherick is Dick."

"I guessed as much, Mr. Manktelow."

"Your lordship is very good. If I may now turn to the settlement. . . ."

Pettigrew had no settlement to turn to, but he was able to follow the story adequately enough from Manktelow's narrative. All the older characters in the pedigree, with their picturesque scriptural names, were long since dead. The proceedings concerned the trust created years before by Samuel, the oldest and, no doubt, by far the wealthiest of the Gormans. It was his hand that stretched out from the grave to manipulate the destinies of his descendants and collaterals.

Clearly, Samuel had been a believer, as the country phrase goes, in "tying his property up". Indeed, he had tied it up about as tightly as the law allowed. In the process of doing so, he had shewn a complete disregard for the interests of the female members of the family. So far as this document was concerned, they might not have existed. His object appeared to have been to preserve the property intact and to preserve it in the male line. Like every lawyer, Pettigrew had met with this unamiable eccentricity before, but there was a peculiarity about these particular dispositions which he did not understand until Manktelow made it clear.

"I may summarize the limitations in the settlement as follows," he said: "to his son Gilbert for his life, and on Gilbert's death to his brother Eli for his life. On Eli's death——"

"Can you explain, Mr. Manktelow, why there is no provision for Gilbert's children? I am aware that in the event he died unmarried, but he was only a young man at the time of the settlement, and the settlor must surely have contemplated that he would have issue."

"My lord, that is exactly what the settlor did not contemplate. As the result of a disease of the kidneys contracted in his youth Gilbert was rendered to all intents incapable of marriage, and his father in making the settlement disregarded the possibility."

Re Gorman, Deceased

"I see. Pray continue."

"If your lordship pleases. On Eli's death, then, the property is to go to Eli's eldest and other sons successively in tail male. I shall have occasion to say something on what I submit is the effect of that provision in the events that have happened, but at this point I should draw your lordship's attention to the fact that Eli, who was of course alive at the date of the settlement, died before his brother Samuel, and that he in fact left one son only, Jack."

"So far, then, the effect of the settlement is—to Gilbert for life and on his decease to Jack."

"To Jack in tail male, my lord."

"Yes, yes, of course. Please go on, Mr. Manktelow, and don't waste time."

"Your lordship is very good. Proceeding, then, we find that the settlement provides that on the failure of Eli's—that is to say Jack's—male issue the property is to be settled upon the junior line. The limitation is similar —to Job for his life and upon Job's death to his eldest and other sons successively in tail. And once more the position is simplified by the fact that Job predeceased his brother Samuel, and left one son only—Dick."

The Judge yawned.

"It all seems remarkably simple, Mr. Manktelow, so far. I don't at the moment appreciate why it should be a matter of concern whether or not Gilbert predeceased Jack. The limitation being to males, and Jack having left daughters only . . ."

"I think that your lordship will see the significance of the question when I tell your lordship that two years

133

ago, that is to say during the lifetime of Gilbert and without his consent, Jack by deed barred his entail."

Once, many years before, Pettigrew had had the good fortune to find himself in the company of an aged ornithologist at the very moment when a hoopoe descended from the sky on to the lawn outside his drawing-room window. He had never forgotten the varied expressions on his face at that moment—the look of blank incredulity merging into excitement as certainty succeeded doubt, the excitement itself subsiding into blissful contentment at the achievement of a lifelong ambition. With astonishment he realized that Manktelow's prosaic words had produced exactly the same effect on Mr. Justice Pomeroy as the hoopoe had on the birdman all those years ago.

"Barred the entail, Mr. Manktelow?" he was saying. "Is it your case that Jack *created a base fee*?"

Manktelow was smiling proudly. It was his hoopoe, all right, there was not a doubt of it. "Precisely, my lord," he said.

"Bless my soul! A base fee! How remarkable! I don't know when I last—— A base fee! This is really very interesting indeed! Pray go on."

I wish, thought Pettigrew, that I had paid more attention to those lectures on real property when I was a student. I wish I had gone into Chancery chambers— no, I don't really, of course, but I wish I had at least learnt a little about what goes on inside them. Above all, if I am to give evidence in this damnable piece of litigation, I wish somebody would condescend to tell me what it is all about.

Re Gorman, Deceased

Even as he suppressed an insane desire to jump up and demand an explanation, there was an interruption from a bench behind him. Mrs. Gorman, untrammelled by the inhibitions that kept Pettigrew speechless, was doing that precise thing.

"Excuse me," she said in her quiet but forceful voice, "but what are you talking about? You've been saying a lot, but it doesn't *mean* anything—not to me, it doesn't. Of course I've known about Uncle Sam's money ever since I was married and what he did with it, but all this stuff——"

By this time, the usher, the associate, three solicitor's clerks and both counsel were uniting in an attempt to suppress her. Support for her came from an unexpected quarter. With all the geniality to be expected of a man who has a hoopoe actually under his eyes on his lawn, Mr. Justice Pomeroy not only condoned the interruption but seemed to welcome it.

"Let Mrs. Gorman come forward," he said.

With Mrs. Gorman standing before him in the well of the court, he proceeded: "I quite understand your difficulty, madam. The position is a little complicated and unusual, but it is perfectly clear. Since you have no advocate, let me explain. This property was settled in such a way that on Gilbert Gorman's death it would pass to your husband for his life and on *his* death to his son, if any. If your husband were to die before his cousin, it would go to that son direct, of course."

"I know all about that, sir."

"I am usually addressed as 'my lord', but no matter. Now there is a process known to the law as 'barring an

entail', by which the man in possession—your husband,
let us say, after Gilbert's death—can alter that arrangement, so that the succession to the property is no longer
limited to sons. Once he has barred the entail, he can
leave it to whom he likes—his wife or daughters. Do you
follow me?"

"Indeed I do, sir—my lord. That was what my husband did when he left me two year ago. Made a will,
he did. My father made him do it, so that my little girls
would be looked after. He said if he didn't do that he'd
prosecute him for taking all that money out of his shop."

"Very well. Now comes the really fascinating part of
the story," his lordship continued, licking his lips.
"That is to say—I recognize that its fascination may not
be readily apparent to you, but it is a really interesting
position none the less. The effect of that disposition of
your husband, made in Gilbert's lifetime and without
his consent, was that if he survived Gilbert the property
would pass as he directed by his will, *but if he died before
Gilbert*, it would all go away from his family to the next
in succession, who is his cousin Dick."

"Why?"

"I beg your pardon?"

"I said, Why?—my lord."

"Well, really, I don't know that I can answer that
question. That is the law, and has been for many hun-
dreds of years. You must take it from me that that is so."

"It seems an odd sort of law to me," observed Mrs.
Gorman dispassionately. "After all, Gilbert had been a
sick man for years, no one thought he'd live as long as
he did, and Jack was young and strong as a horse——"

136

Re Gorman, Deceased

"No doubt, madam. That would perhaps explain why your father took the course he did. But those are hardly circumstances that affect the position in law."

"I suppose not."

Mrs. Gorman looked very lonely, standing there looking up at the bench. As though for the first time Pettigrew realized that she was the only woman in that assemblage of men. At the same time, he realized something else that gave him the answer to a lot of problems.

"May I ask you one question, my lord?"

"Certainly."

"If this child I'm carrying now turns out to be a boy, what happens to the money then?"

"Edna!"

Mr. Joliffe, who up to that moment had been sitting listlessly watching the proceedings as though they did not concern him, suddenly rose to his feet, his face scarlet.

"You shameless girl——" he began. He got no further.

"Sit down," said Mr. Justice Pomeroy.

He spoke quietly, but Mr. Joliffe sat down as though his legs had been pulled from under him, his red face suddenly pale.

His lordship turned to Mrs. Gorman as though the interruption had not occurred.

"I understood you to say that your husband left you two years ago," he said.

"True enough, my lord. But he came to me on the Friday night, the night before he was killed. It wasn't the first time either, though my father never knew. He

wanted money, of course—he always did—and I had
little enough to give him. But he was my husband, and
what I had, I gave."

"What you had, you gave?" the Judge repeated
quietly. "I see."

There was silence in the court for a moment. Pettigrew was seeing once more the farmyard of Sallowcombe in the half-light of dawn and the blended
shadows of a man and a woman at the window opposite
his own. He marvelled that he should ever have been so
blind as not to guess the truth.

"Mr. Manktelow," said the Judge, "this raises rather
an interesting question, does it not?"

"My lord, it does. This has taken me entirely by surprise. I need hardly say that those instructing me were
quite unaware——"

"So I should have imagined."

"If your lordship would be good enough to grant an
adjournment to allow me to consider the position . . ."

"I don't see the necessity for an adjournment, Mr.
Manktelow. The situation is unusual and involved, but
I think it is perfectly clear. If this child proves to be a
girl, nothing is changed. Matters remain *in statu quo
ante*. But if it should be a boy"—Mr. Justice Pomeroy
licked his lips—"it is a really delightfully complex proposition, Mr. Manktelow—he will *preserve the base fee* for
his mother's enjoyment, will he not?"

"I should apprehend so, my lord."

"Preserve it, that is, so long as he lives——" he went
on in a rising tone of excitement. Manktelow caught his
mood, and chimed in:

Re Gorman, Deceased

"And he has only to live till he is twelve years old——"

"Just so. The Limitation Act, 1939——"

"Section 11, my lord——"

"And in that case his mother's interest will become——"

"Indefeasible!"

The two men, smiling broadly, chanted the last word in perfect unison. Under a capable producer, Pettigrew thought, they could have made a reasonably good pair of cross-talk comedians. Then Mr. Justice Pomeroy abruptly recovered his dignity and said:

"I shall not grant an adjournment."

"As your lordship pleases."

Turning to Mrs. Gorman, he said, "The answer to your question, madam, as you may have gathered, is that the sex of your child may make a considerable difference. When is it expected, by the way?"

"The third week in June, my lord."

"You have not so very long to wait, then. If it is a boy, the property is yours so long as he lives, and yours for good should he survive to the age of twelve."

"Thank you, my lord. And now that is settled, may I go away?"

"But nothing is settled. I still have to try this case."

"I don't see what there is to try."

"Don't you understand? Whether you have a son or another daughter, this property is yours already, under your husband's will, unless the Plaintiff, Mr. Dick Gorman, can prove that your husband died on Saturday, the 9th of September and not on Tuesday, the 12th."

Re Gorman, Deceased

"He needn't bother to prove that," said Mrs. Gorman sadly. "Jack died on Saturday, the morning he left me. I've known it all along."

"The Death Certificate before me certifies that he died on Tuesday, and that remains the date of his death until the contrary is proved. I have to hear the evidence."

"He died on Saturday," Mrs. Gorman repeated, and for the first time there was passion in her voice. "And how he died no one will tell me, though there's someone here knows well enough, I think. And Gilbert, that had lain a-dying for months, lingered on till Sunday. That's how it was. The gentleman said right when he told you the coroner and all were deceived, my lord. But I was deceived, too. My Jack was hidden away till after Gilbert was dead, and then brought out to be found again with his wounds all fresh as though he had only just died. It's that I can't get out of my mind—my husband's poor body shut up in a butcher's cold store like the carcase of a sheep or a steer, so that his daughters would get what wasn't rightly theirs. It doesn't seem possible, but there's those will do anything for money. And that's the truth, my lord. Ask my father if it's not the truth!"

CHAPTER XIV

According to the Evidence

Edna Gorman's voice trailed away into a silence that lasted just long enough to give Pettigrew time to wonder what was the appropriate Chancery reaction to these very untypical Chancery proceedings. Then Mr. Justice Pomeroy supplied the answer. He raised his heavy-lidded eyes towards the time-piece on the wall, heaved himself out of his chair and observed to the assembled company, now respectfully upstanding, "Two o'clock." The morning had gone; it was time to be thinking of lunch.

In the corridor outside the court, Pettigrew felt his arm being taken in a firm but friendly grip. He looked round, and saw that it was Manktelow.

"I'm not sure that I want to talk to you," said Pettigrew.

"Don't be silly. Of course you do. You're my witness."

"What you mean is, that you want to talk to me."

"You will find that it comes to exactly the same thing. You will be lunching in hall. So shall I. You will sit at the same table you have used since you were called. So shall I. I shall come and sit next to you and you will have no escape. You had better accept your fate quietly."

Pettigrew surrendered. Manktelow, after all, was a man and a brother. Chancery had long since claimed him for her own, but he was none the less a Templar of the same Inn as Pettigrew. They had lunched together, with intervals for two world wars and other interruptions, fairly regularly for over forty years. Since Pettigrew retired from practice after the second war, they had neither met nor corresponded, but this did not prevent them from taking up their acquaintance exactly where they had left it. They walked together to the robing-room, and it seemed odd and unnatural that only one of them should have a wig and gown to leave behind there. Together they strolled across the Strand, in the wake of a judge for whom a policeman was holding up the traffic. It was all deliciously like old times. Then they went into hall.

"Hall" to Pettigrew meant a lofty stone building in Victorian Gothic, panelled with highly varnished wood, adorned with the escutcheons of by-gone celebrities and nonentities, and populated by large statues representing the nineteenth-century's idea of medieval Knights Templar. Aesthetes had condemned it; Hitler had destroyed it; Pettigrew missed it very much. The familiar table was still in the same place, with the familiar faces around it. He noticed that one or two strangers had contrived not only to get themselves called to the Bar, but to insinuate themselves among his friends, but he was prepared for a reasonable amount of change in ten years. What he was not prepared for was the babel of sound that assailed his ears as he entered the shining, new, handsome building that was now "hall". Everybody seemed to be shouting at the top of his voice. The clatter of knives and forks was deafening. The feet of the waiters hurrying across the floor thundered like charging cavalry.

"What's happened to everyone?" Pettigrew bellowed to Manktelow. "I can't hear myself speak."

"Didn't you know?" His voice came to Pettigrew with difficulty through the hubbub. "It's something they call acoustics. Apparently this sort of floor and this kind of ceiling put together in a room this shape are guaranteed to produce this result. It's a very interesting scientific demonstration. You're jolly lucky to have heard it. They'll do something to the place soon and spoil it."

Pettigrew shook his head mournfully.

"I thought you wanted to *talk*," he said.

"Yes I do. Eat up quickly and we'll have time for a stroll round the garden."

"What exactly are you going to say?" Manktelow asked as they walked across the great lawn.

"Hasn't Mallett told you? Simply that I saw what appeared to be the body of a man on Bolter's Tussock on the afternoon of Saturday the whatever-it-was, and when I came back later it wasn't there."

"What appeared to be?"

"That's as far as I shall go."

"H'm. I shall be producing a photograph of the body that certainly was there on the Tuesday morning. Do you think you will be able to identify it?"

"I might and I might not. But you're not telling me that that's the only evidence you've got to connect the two?"

"No, it's not."

"I thought not," said Pettigrew.

"Why didn't you tell the police what you had seen?" Manktelow asked.

"That's cross-examination. If Twentyman asks me that, I suppose I shall have to answer, but I'm damned if I tell you."

They turned under the plane trees overlooking the Embankment and started to walk back over the grass.

"You don't seem to be interested in the case," observed Manktelow reproachfully, after they had gone some way in silence.

"On the contrary, I am very much interested, and I badly want to know, but I don't suppose you can tell me. Who or what killed Jack Gorman? Have you any ideas?"

"Good lord, no! The question never even crossed my mind."

"It's an interesting question, all the same, you know."

"I dare say it is," said Manktelow impatiently. "For those who care for such things. But it's not my case. Not the case you're giving evidence in. Aren't you interested in that?"

"Dash it all, I've already heard you open it in court at some considerable length, and you and Mrs. Gorman between you have really told me all I need to know about it. Incidentally, unless we walk up, we shan't be there on time. It's getting late." They quickened their pace as they left the garden and began to thread the Temple courts.

"But this is ridiculous," spluttered Manktelow. He was stout and not in the best of condition, and the pace that Pettigrew had set was rather too much for him. "This is a remarkable case—a unique one, I should not be afraid to say, using the word for once in its strict and proper meaning. You could see for yourself how excited Puffkins was over it."

"If by Puffkins you mean the Honourable Mr. Justice Pomeroy, I can only say that his ideas of excitement are not mine. I'm too old to start getting enthusiastic about base fees."

They had emerged from the Temple precincts on to the pavement opposite the Royal Courts of Justice.

"You're damnably cold-blooded," said Manktelow. "For six months you must have been wondering how you came to see a dead man three days before he died. Now you know the answer, you pretend not to be interested."

"We've only got three minutes," said Pettigrew, looking up at the great clock. He plunged boldly on to the crossing, a protesting Manktelow beside him. "For six months," he went on, "I've been running away from this case because it seemed to me irrational and, worse than irrational, thoroughly frightening." He landed on the other side, sprinted with Manktelow to the robing-room door, and went on, "Never mind why I was frightened—I haven't time to give you the history of my

145

childhood now, and it's none of your business. But as soon as I saw your sub poena, I realized that there must be a perfectly rational explanation to the whole thing." He helped Manktelow on with his gown. "Now that I know what it is, I feel a fool not to have seen it before; but as I say, I wasn't looking for it. On the contrary, I was looking away from it as hard as I could."

They started on the narrow stairs up to the court corridor. Manktelow had his second wind by now and trotted up first.

"You ought to be feeling relieved, anyway," he threw over his shoulder. "This case will have solved the problem."

Pettigrew caught him up in the corridor.

"I don't know what you call solving the problem," he panted. "You're going to persuade Puffkins to deliver a judgment which will disinherit Mrs. Gorman's charming little daughters, if you're not pipped on the post by a posthumous son. Great fun for all of you, and costs out of the estate. But it doesn't satisfy me. Because now I have been compelled to look at this case again I feel that as sure as God made little apples there's been murder done here, and nobody's got within a mile of solving *that* problem yet."

They reached Chancery Court VI just as Puffkins, punctual to the second, was taking his seat. Pettigrew made his way to his inconspicuous post at the back of the court, but he never reached it.

"My lord, I call Mr. Pettigrew," said Manktelow with an evil grin, and thrust his hapless friend, still gasping for breath, straight into the witness-box.

According to the Evidence

On the whole, the experience was not quite so bad a one as Pettigrew had bargained for. At least, nobody referred to the possibility of precognition. None the less, he had some awkward passages to surmount.

"On the afternoon of Saturday the 9th of September," Manktelow asked him, "were you at the place known as Bolter's Tussock?"

Pettigrew agreed that he was, and after some business with a large-scale Ordnance Survey map identified the exact spot.

"You were on horseback, I think?"

"Er—yes. That is . . ."

"Well, were you or weren't you?" interjected the judge. "You must know."

"It was a pony, my lord."

"Very well—on ponyback. Don't quibble, Mr. Pettigrew. Please get on, Mr. Manktelow."

"I am much obliged to your lordship. And as you reached this point did you see something on the ground?"

"I thought I did, yes."

"Just look at this photograph, will you, Mr. Pettigrew? Does it appear to you to resemble in any way the object which you saw on the ground?"

"He hasn't said he saw anything," his lordship pointed out. "He says he thought he saw something."

"Your lordship is very good. Looking at the photograph, do you now say whether you saw anything, and if so what?"

There is nothing in the world quite so definite and uncompromising as a police photograph. Jack Gorman's

147

face stared at Pettigrew from the print and told him very plainly that he could take it or leave it, but that there must be no shilly-shallying. He chose to take it.

"I saw this man on the ground," he said firmly. "But my impression is that he was not in this position, exactly."

"Your impression?" said the Judge.

"My lord, I only saw him for a very short time. I— that is, I . . ."

"You rode off at once to get help, did you not, Mr. Pettigrew?" said Manktelow.

"Yes, I did," Pettigrew hoped that his gratitude for the suggestion was not too apparent in his voice. But something apparently had put Mr. Justice Pomeroy on enquiry.

"You didn't get down to have a look at him first?" he asked incredulously.

"No, my lord, I didn't." It was on the tip of his tongue to say frankly that he didn't because he couldn't, but something inhibited him. An Englishman will always prefer an imputation on his morals to one on his horse-manship. Who had said that? Dr. Johnson? Surtees? Oscar Wilde? His perplexity must have shewn itself on his face, for Manktelow hastened to come to his aid.

"Would it be right to say that you were in a hurry to get assistance as soon as you could?"

"Oh, absolutely." Pettigrew offered up silent thanks to counsel prepared to put such a leading question and to the judge who allowed it. But his relief was only temporary.

148

"And then you returned later with help—how much later would you say, Mr. Pettigrew?"

"I'm not sure exactly—perhaps half an hour. Perhaps a little more."

"Half an hour!" Pomeroy rolled round in his seat to stare at the witness. "I thought you said you were in a hurry?"

"My lord," said Manktelow, boldly intervening, "I am given to understand that this is a somewhat remote spot. Your lordship will see from the map that the nearest habitation is——"

"It's within a few yards of a busy main road," retorted his lordship. "However, if the witness is saying that it took him half an hour to fetch help—— That is what you are saying, is it, sir?"

"Yes, my lord."

"—well, if that is what he says, Mr. Manktelow, I suppose I must accept it, for what it is worth."

"If your lordship pleases. And when you did return, was there anything there?"

"There was not."

"The body had gone?"

"Yes."

At this point, Pettigrew realized why it was that Pomeroy, J. was familiarly known to those who practised before him as Puffkins. For his lordship's face quite suddenly altered its shape altogether. He took a deep breath and inflated his cheeks until they stood out like the two halves of a round, pink ball. He maintained this attitude for an appreciable time before expelling the air from his lungs in a long sigh that seemed to

149

express better than any words could have done his deep
distrust of everything that he had heard from the witness-box.

"And after witnessing this disappearing trick on the
part of the corpse," he asked Pettigrew, "what did you
then do?"

It was the question that Pettigrew had been dreading
ever since he had entered the witness-box. If it had not
been put to him in such an offensive way, and by a
man whose facial antics he thought extremely ridiculous, he might have found difficulty in answering it.
Now, he felt a sudden surge of anger and contempt, and
under the spur of his emotions he said the first thing
that came into his head—which happened to be the
exact truth.

"I went to bed for two days with a high temperature," he said, and he contrived to put into his tone
exactly what he was feeling.

Puffkins gave him a long, hard look. Then, astonishingly, he smiled.

"I'm not altogether surprised," he said. "And when
you finally got out of bed, you decided that nobody was
likely to believe you. That does not surprise me either.
After all, I have had some difficulty in believing you
myself. But I do believe you, Mr. Pettigrew. Thank you,
Mr. Manktelow. Do you cross-examine, Mr. Twentyman?"

Twentyman's cross-examination was little more than a
formality, and Pettigrew escaped thankfully from the box.

"My lord," said Manktelow, "my next witness is
Detective-Inspector Parkinson."

According to the Evidence

The Judge looked disappointed. "I hoped it was going to be Mr. Joliffe," he said.

"My lord, my clients have elected not to call him. They were conscious of the probability that Mr. Joliffe might object to answering questions tending to incriminate himself——"

Mr. Justice Pomeroy, who was something of an antiquarian, murmured something about exhibiting a pardon under the Great Seal.

"I think that I shall be in a position to satisfy your lordship without recourse to that. The police officer in the course of his investigations has taken a statement in writing from Mr. Joliffe——"

"I shan't admit it. Why should I? It's only secondary evidence at the best, and the man who made the statement is actually in court."

"None the less, if your lordship will be good enough to hear the officer, I think that those parts of his evidence which are plainly admissible will make it abundantly clear——"

By this time the hapless Parkinson, waiting to take the oath, had become horribly nervous. He was used to holding his local Petty Sessions in the hollow of his hand; Recorders and even Judges of Assize he could confront with assurance; but the mysterious proceedings of the High Court of Chancery filled him with alarm. The first ten minutes of his evidence, therefore, punctuated as they were by caustic comments from the Bench and by two or three successful objections from Twentyman, were thoroughly unhappy. But after that things improved. Pomeroy began to be impressed by the story that Parkinson had to tell, and when the officer produced a highly technical report from the Forensic Science Laboratory, with accompanying exhibits, he was completely captivated. It is not every day that a Judge of the Chancery Division finds himself plunged into the hurly-burly of police work, and Puffkins forgot even the refined delights of the base fee in contemplation of detection in real life.

"Fascinating, fascinating!" he murmured, toying with a magnifying glass. "Let me see that I have this right, Inspector. The contents of envelope 'A' are fragments of sawdust from the cold store of Mr. Joliffe's butcher's shop; the contents of envelope 'B', dust and other material from the floor of Mr. Joliffe's van; the contents of envelope 'C' consists of material taken from the deceased's jacket, consisting partly of sawdust identical with exhibit 'A', partly of dust identical with exhibit 'B'. 'A', 'B' and 'C' alike are impregnated with blood, which, on analysis, proves to be animal, but not human."

"Quite right, my lord."

"Good! Now let me see if I appreciate the significance of the button. That was found at Satcherley Way, I think you said?"

"About half a mile to the west of Satcherley Way, my lord. On the edge of the road."

"A button identical with those on the deceased's clothing. Your theory is that the deceased met his death at that spot. How, by the way?"

"I'm not in a position to say, my lord."

"Pity. Never mind, that is a side issue. Having died

there, he was taken to the cold store, *via* Bolter's Tussock. Curious, that. Why stop half-way?"

"Mr. Joliffe's statement, my lord——"

"Tut, tut! I can't have that. If you can't answer the question, you can't answer it. Now can you answer this one? Granted that you can prove that the body was in the van and in the cold store, how do you prove that it was there before Sunday, when Mr. Gilbert Gorman died?"

"The butcher's premises were shut from the close of business on Saturday until Tuesday morning, my lord. If the body didn't get in there by Saturday evening, it didn't get there at all."

Mr. Justice Pomeroy nodded. Then he looked at the clock. A tidy-minded man, he disliked leaving the fag-end of a case to be finished on the second day. At the same time, he disliked sitting beyond his accustomed time.

"Well, Mr. Twentyman?" he said.

"If your lordship will allow me one moment," said Twentyman.

He consulted briefly with the solicitors instructing him and then announced that on behalf of the trustees of the settlement he did not propose to contest the case any further. Subject to his costs being provided for, he was prepared to consent to the declaration claimed by the Plaintiff.

"Very well, Mr. Twentyman. I think you are wise. There will be a declaration as prayed."

Mrs. Gorman stood up.

"Then who has won the day, my lord?" she asked.

According to the Evidence

"Mr. Dick Gorman has won the day, madam, just as you said he would. Whether his victory is any profit to him depends on what happens on another day—in the third week in June, I think you said?"

Mrs. Gorman nodded silently and walked out of court. Pettigrew, following her with his eyes, was pleased to see Dick Gorman catch her up and engage her in what seemed a friendly conversation. Mr. Joliffe followed them out, and turned down the corridor in the opposite direction. He was quite alone.

CHAPTER XV

Post-mortem in Fleet Street

Pettigrew did not wait to talk to Manktelow or to Mallett, or to anyone else. He felt suddenly in urgent need of fresh air, and made his way straight out of the building. Once beyond the doors, he halted, irresolute. Eleanor, he suddenly remembered, had decided to come to London to join Hester Greenway, who was making one of her very rare descents on the metropolis on some obscure expedition. Had he arranged to meet Eleanor, and if so, where and when? Feeling thoroughly stupid, he dawdled there, his mind a complete blank, while homing barristers, witnesses and solicitors' clerks swirled past him.

"Well, Frank! Thank goodness you waited for us— I thought we were never going to get out of that place."

Pettigrew turned to see his wife coming towards him, accompanied by a weatherbeaten woman who could only be Hester Greenway.

"Where do you come from?" he asked in surprise.

"From the public gallery in the Court, of course. Do you mean to say you never saw us?"

"No," said Pettigrew rather shaken. "I didn't." As a good witness should, he had turned towards the bench to give his evidence. The public gallery, in any event, was the last place to which a man of his training would think of giving his attention. "You never told me you were coming," he added reproachfully.

"I didn't know I was. It was Hester's idea. Oh, that reminds me——"

She introduced her husband to Hester in due form.

"I thought you put up a jolly good show," said Hester, shaking Pettigrew's hand warmly. "I wanted to clap, but Ellie said I'd only put you off. Do tell me one thing, though. Did the pony bolt with you?"

"It did," said Pettigrew. "How did you know?" To his great surprise, he found himself thinking that he was going to like Miss Greenway very much.

"Well, for one thing, those Gorman ponies always will if you give them half a chance. Mind you, I don't blame you for not telling the judge, when he was asking all those silly questions, but I think he ought to have guessed that was why you didn't stop to look at the body."

"It's not the only thing he ought to have guessed," remarked Eleanor.

Hester smiled at Eleanor, and Eleanor smiled at Hester. It was the kind of smile that passes between people of superior intelligence in the presence of a deplorably ignorant third party.

"Well?" said Pettigrew. "What ought he to have guessed?"

"That Mrs. Gorman was going to have a baby, of course. It was *obvious*. We spotted it the moment we saw her."

156

Post-mortem in Fleet Street

"It wasn't only the judge, it was the whole lot of you,"
observed Hester. " 'My lord, this has taken me entirely
by surprise'." She gave a very passable imitation of
Manktelow's manner. "I never saw a crowd of men
look so silly. Two of them detectives, too! Mr. Parkinson!" she called out, suddenly. "Don't go, Mr. Parkinson. I've something I wanted to ask you."

Inspector Parkinson, with Mallett by his side, was
just leaving the Law Courts. He stopped and took off
his hat to Hester.

"I wasn't expecting to see you here, Miss Greenway," he said.

"Never mind what you were expecting. It's what
Edna Gorman's expecting that we were talking about.
Didn't either you or Mr. Mallett guess?"

"To tell you the truth, ma'am, we hadn't given it a
thought. And now, if you'll excuse us——"

"Of course I won't excuse you. There are dozens
of things I want to hear about, and so does Mrs.
Pettigrew. Mr. Pettigrew, isn't there somewhere near
here where we can get some tea? I don't know about
anyone else, but I'm simply dying for a cup."

"It's very kind of you, Miss Greenway, but I really
ought to be getting along."

"Well, if you must, Inspector, I suppose you must.
But I thought you told me the other day that you
wanted one of Jeannie's puppies . . . ?"

So it was that to his great surprise Pettigrew found
himself playing host to a party of five in a Fleet Street
teashop. It was a somewhat constrained party at

157

first, but once he had persuaded Mallett that he bore him no malice the atmosphere became friendly enough.

"The first thing *I* want to know is," said Hester Greenway, as soon as the cups had been poured out, "When are you prosecuting that odious creature Joliffe?"

"What do you suggest he should be prosecuted for, ma'am?" asked the Inspector cautiously.

"Good gracious, I don't know. That's your business, not mine. Making a fool of the coroner, I suppose."

"I'm afraid that's not an offence known to the law, ma'am."

"But he must have done *something!*"

"I can't help thinking Miss Greenway is right," Pettigrew put in. "I'm deplorably rusty in these matters, but might I suggest that our old friend, a Common Law Misdemeanour——"

"Against the Peace of our Sovereign Lady the Queen, her Crown and Dignity." Mallett rolled the phrase lovingly round his tongue.

"Exactly. There must have been something like this before at some time."

"Rather over a hundred years ago, sir," said Parkinson. "You'll have heard of the Resurrection men, no doubt."

"Then you have considered a prosecution?" said Pettigrew.

"It was not a matter for me to consider, sir. I reported the matter to the Chief Constable and he took the advice of the Director of Public Prosecutions. And the decision was—not to prosecute."

"Why on earth not?" asked Hester.

"I rather think that some doubt was felt as to whether a conviction would be secured in such an unusual class of case."

Something in the Inspector's tone put Eleanor on enquiry. "Was that the only reason for not prosecuting him?" she asked. "Or was there something else?"

"Well, madam, now that you have raised the subject —this is in strict confidence, of course—there was at one time the possibility that Joliffe might be prosecuted on a graver charge."

Inspector Parkinson's face was brick red from the strain of endeavouring to combine civility with his sense of police propriety.

"You thought he'd murdered Jack?"

"Really, madam, I haven't said that. It would be most improper of me——"

"He could have done it easily in a fit of temper, and then remembered that it wouldn't pay him," Eleanor went on, sublimely regardless of the Inspector's embarrassment. "Or not murdered him—just manslaughtered him in his car by accident."

"Jack Gorman wasn't killed by Mr. Joliffe's car," Parkinson volunteered. "As a matter of fact, I shouldn't be surprised if it wasn't a car at all."

"Steady on!" said Hester. "We all read what the doctor said at the inquest."

"That doctor was a——" Parkinson hesitated, turned a darker shade of red and shut his mouth firmly. He opened it again to swallow down the last of his tea, and then with a mumbled apology left the teashop.

"Well! If he thinks he's going to get a pup from me after that . . ." was Hester's disgusted comment.

Pettigrew's reaction to the Inspector's disappearance was different. "Mr. Mallett," he said, "when you were a Detective-Inspector did you discuss cases with members of the public?"

"I did not, sir."

"Now that you are no longer in the force, do you feel at liberty to discuss this case with us?"

"I think so, sir, yes."

"Then in that case, I think we should be grateful to Parkinson for taking himself off. I take it that everything he knows about this case, you know?"

Mallett hesitated. He was a modest man, but he had a high regard for truth.

"I think that would be an under-statement, sir," he said.

"Excellent! That is all I need to know about Parkinson. Will you therefore please take another of those sugar cakes and give your mind to the following questions: When, where, why, how and by whom was Jack Gorman killed?"

Mallett demolished the cake in astonishingly quick time, brushed the crumbs out of his moustache and said, "*When?* Within fairly narrow limits, that presents no particular difficulty now. On this Saturday morning Jack Gorman must have left his wife early——"

"I can help you there. I saw him. It was just day-break."

"That means that he was alive about half past five Greenwich mean time, or half past six by the clock. If

Post-mortem in Fleet Street

Mr. Joliffe is telling the truth, and I think he is in this matter, he was dead by half past seven, which was when he found him while on his way to work that morning."

"Very well. That brings us logically to *Where?*"

"Assuming that he was killed where Joliffe says that he found him—two assumptions this time, sir, but they seem to be reasonable ones—we can determine that exactly. I don't know whether you know Satcherley Copse, sir?"

Pettigrew closed his eyes and delved back into his distant memories once more. There came to him a recollection of waiting in a chilling wind and icy rain while hounds were hopelessly at fault in a tangle of neglected woodland. The pony coughed twice on the way home, and he was sick with fear that it would be unfit to ride the next hunting day. Yes he knew Satcherley Copse.

"It's a hanging wood above Stinchcombe Water," he said.

"Quite right, sir. And you get to it from the road by a gate near the top of Gallows Hill. That's the direct road from Sallowcombe to Whitsea, of course. Joliffe found his son-in-law by that gate, his head and shoulders in the road, his feet towards the gate—which was open, incidentally, he says. I've been over the ground since, both with and without Mr. Parkinson, and, as you know, we did find Jack's button. Apart from that, by the time we got there, there were no traces left. In any case, I should think that by midday on that same Saturday anything in the road or near it had been hopelessly obscured. Besides cars on the road, there must have been a couple of hundred horses at least through that gate within a few hours of Joliffe finding him."

"Of course. The meet was at Satcherley Way that morning."

"Yes, sir. And Mr. Olding tells me that the stag was roused in Satcherley Copse."

"In that case, the ground must have been a mass of hoofprints. So far so good. We've dealt with When and Where, but now I want to go to *Why*? And Why isn't single here, but double or triple. First Why: Why was Jack Gorman on Gallows Hill at all?"

"It's within easy walking distance of Sallowcombe, sir, and he had to go somewhere when he left. Other than that, I can't suggest why he should have gone in that particular direction."

Hester Greenway chuckled.

"I can," she said. "He was within a mile of Highbarn Farm."

"Highbarn Farm?" said Mallett in surprise. "Tom Gorman's place, do you mean?"

"Certainly that's what I mean."

"But what should he be going there for?"

"What should anybody be going anywhere for at that hour of the morning? For breakfast, of course."

"You think that Jack Gorman expected Tom to give him breakfast?"

Miss Greenway clicked her tongue in impatience at the denseness of the man.

"Not Tom, of course. Everybody on the moor knows he couldn't stand the sight of him. He wouldn't have given him a crust of bread. But Ethel would."

"Who is Ethel?" asked Eleanor.

"Tom's wife, Dick's sister, Jack's cousin—she'd give him breakfast or—or—anything else he cared to ask for. So would nine women out of ten in a twenty mile radius. Surely you knew that, Mr. Mallett?"

"I knew Jack Gorman had a certain reputation as a lady's man, miss, but I'm bound to say it never occurred to me. You may be right, of course, but if he went to Highbarn, how was he to avoid meeting Tom?"

"It was a hunting day, wasn't it? And Tom was acting as harbourer while the regular man was ill. That meant he'd be up and out of the place hours before. No—Jack's only trouble would be to finish his breakfast before Tom came back for his. But he was pretty expert at dodging husbands, was Jack. He was a character and no mistake!"

Hester concluded her obituary of Jack Gorman with an indulgent laugh, in which Pettigrew joined and Eleanor rather pointedly did not.

"Well," said Pettigrew, "we've got a fairly plausible answer to that question, at all events. My next one comes back to Joliffe. According to his story, having found the body, he immediately decides to conceal it. Why?"

"Because he knows that Gilbert is dying, sir, and he's thinking of this base fee business if it is known that Jack has died first."

"Is he, by Jove? Then he's a very learned butcher. I'm a lawyer, or used to be, and I shouldn't know the first thing about it if Puffkins hadn't expounded it in words of one syllable."

"I can explain that quite easily, sir. When he made Jack bar the entail, he was warned by the lawyer that advised him, of the importance of Jack surviving Gilbert. But of course nobody then ever imagined that he wouldn't."

"So much for that. Now for the next question. Having found Jack, he apparently just dumped him off the road at Bolter's Tussock, where he wouldn't be seen. Why didn't he take him down and pop him into the deep freeze at once?"

"He couldn't do that. He's only got a little two-seater car. How would he have looked arriving at his business with a corpse on the passenger seat?"

"Granted. But at least I should have expected him to come back in double quick time with the van. Instead, he waited till late in the afternoon, which couldn't have done Jack much good, considering the weather."

"There's good reason for that. It wasn't until the afternoon that he could get his shop and cold store to himself. I got some very interesting information from Joliffe's shop assistant about what happened on Saturday. Joliffe had to choose his time carefully, so that he would be back in the place after the staff had gone. I don't know what excuse he intended to give for taking the van out after the normal delivery times, but he had a bit of luck in the shape of a last-minute S.O.S. for meat from a local hotel. He told his driver that rather than keep him working late on overtime rates he'd do the job himself. So he left the assistant in charge of the shop, took the meat to the hotel, collected poor Jack, and timed himself to get back to the shop after everyone had gone."

Hester clapped her hands suddenly.

"Of course!" she exclaimed. "And he told us just the opposite!"

"Told you what, miss?"

"Don't you remember, Ellie? That afternoon when you came to see me and your car broke down, Mr. Joliffe said he couldn't give you a lift home because he had to be back in the shop before closing time. The sly old sinner, that was exactly what he didn't want to be!"

"He did give us a lift, as a matter of fact," said Eleanor, "though it was only a couple of hundred yards or so." She shuddered. "And Jack must have been in the back of the van then."

Hester gave a hoot of laughter.

"And I offered to get into the back and sit with the meat, because we were so squashed in front!" she exclaimed. "That must have given him a turn. No wonder he didn't take to the suggestion!".

"This is all news to me," said Mallett. "I had no idea that you had met Joliffe that afternoon. What happened, exactly?"

Hester told him briefly what had occurred.

"I thought he had just looked in at Minster to make

passes at Louisa as usual," she concluded. "But obviously he was killing time as well. To think I had only to open the back of the van and shew the old villain up—it makes me mad!"

"Making passes at Louisa?" asked Pettigrew. "Is that one of our friend's weaknesses?"

"It certainly used to be. He was always dropping in at the Grange—tempting her with choice steaks and slabs of liver, I shouldn't wonder—but he must have cooled off lately. I haven't seen him about since Ellie and I had our ride with the corpse."

"This is an interesting digression," said Pettigrew, "but I want to get back to my questions. We still have to tackle the ones that really matter—*How?* and *By Whom?*"

Mallett shook his head. "I wish I could answer those ones, sir," he said.

"But this is absurd. There must be an answer. After all, there's plenty of evidence available, one way and another. Let's go over it together once more. . . ."

For some time, Pettigrew had been vaguely aware that the tea-shop, which had been crowded when they entered, was emptying rapidly. He had also known that his wife was making signs to him indicating that he should either do something or refrain from whatever it was that he happened to be doing. He had disregarded both phenomena, the one because it did not concern him, the other from established habit. Now he met with an interruption which he could not disregard.

Post-mortem in Fleet Street

"Excuse me, sir, but will you be requiring anything else, because we are closing now?"

The waitress was kind but firm. Rather sheepishly, he took the bill that she gave him and made his way to the cash desk through a forest of empty tables and upturned chairs. He turned to find his party in a state of dissolution. Hester was bidding an affectionate farewell of Eleanor and explaining that she had an engagement to spend the evening with the Old Cocky-olly-bird—a name which elicited from Eleanor glad cries of loving recognition. Mallett was extending his hand to say Goodbye. A moment later they were swept out into the street.

Pettigrew saw Miss Greenway into a cruising taxi and turned to Mallett. For the first time he realized that his old friend was now well advanced in years. He looked not only old, but rather tired.

"What are your plans for this evening?" he asked him.

"Mr. Parkinson has asked me to have supper with him and some friends at the Yard," said Mallett. He seemed unenthusiastic at the prospect. "I've left my bag at a hotel near Paddington."

Husband and wife exchanged quick glances.

"Why don't you change your mind and come home with us?" asked Pettigrew.

Mallett's face lit up. He turned to Eleanor.

"May I, ma'am?" he asked.

"I wish you would."

"I ought to warn you—if I do, Mr. Pettigrew and I will be talking about this case half the night."

Post-mortem in Fleet Street

"You can talk as much as you like, Mr. Mallett, so long as you arrive at some conclusion, if it's only that there's nothing to be done. I want a little peace and quiet, and I know I shan't have any until this ghost is laid once and for all!"

CHAPTER XVI

The Right Question

"*How?*" said Pettigrew. "*How* and *By Whom?*"

They were sitting in Pettigrew's tiny study at Yewbury, Mallett smoking his pipe, Pettigrew pulling at one of his rare cigars. A decanter, a siphon and two glasses were at hand.

"As to How, sir," said Mallett. "Well, you know what the doctor said at the inquest."

"And I heard what Inspector Parkinson said about the doctor."

"I think the Inspector is a trifle prejudiced about him, sir. Ever since I persuaded him that the medical evidence about the time of the death might be wrong—and what a job I had to get him to consider it!—he won't hear any good of him. And yet all the doctor said was that the injuries were consistent with being knocked down by a car, and so they were."

"It wasn't Joliffe's car, though."

"No doubt about that, sir. It's quite impossible to kill a man with a car without leaving some pretty obvious marks on it, and ninety-nine times out of a hundred you'll smash a headlight as well. There are no such marks on Joliffe's car, and no signs of any recent repairs or painting. What bothers me is that Parkinson's men haven't found any fragments of glass or traces of paint where the body was found by Joliffe, which I should expect if he had been run down by a car." Mallett sipped his whisky and added reflectively, "Unless, of course, he was knocked down somewhere else, and moved afterwards to Satcherley Copse."

"No," said Pettigrew decisively. "No. I absolutely decline to consider any more removals. This corpse is peripatetic enough as it is. You must think of something else."

Mallett shook his head.

"I've only the medical reports and the photographs to go upon," he said. "It's quite clear to my mind that Jack Gorman was run over by a car—there are injuries on the legs and lower parts of the body that couldn't well have been caused in any other way. But those weren't the injuries that killed him. It's my belief that Joliffe ran over the body as it lay on the road. He would have been coming round a bend there and could have done it quite easily by accident, though he won't admit to any such thing."

"And the injuries that killed him?" Pettigrew asked.

"A tremendous blow just over the heart. I'm not sure that it wasn't two blows, but the area of damage was so extensive that it's difficult to be certain. I've tried experiments, and there are several types of car and lorry that could catch a man at just that height with various parts of the wing or bonnet. But it is unusual to find the injury so concentrated as it was in this case."

"So something else than a car could have done it?"

"Yes. A man with a sledge-hammer could have done

it. Or better still, two men, each with a sledge-hammer. It would be rather a job to hit anyone in that particular part of the body if he was standing up, though. Easier if he was lying down."

Mallett spoke in the tone of one discussing improbabilities so wild as to be virtually impossible, but his last phrase evoked a sudden disturbing suggestion in Pettigrew's mind.

"Lying down?" he repeated. "In bed, for instance?"

"Quite so, sir."

"I was thinking about what Miss Greenway had suggested as to Jack's going to Highbarn Farm that morning."

"That had come into my mind also, sir."

"What kind of woman is Ethel Gorman?"

"I only know her by sight, sir. A very attractive young person."

"And Tom Gorman?"

"Well, you've met him yourself, sir, and can form your own opinion. Quiet, reserved, wouldn't you say? I should add, rather secretive." Mallett paused, knocked his pipe out into an ashtray, and went on: "He has the reputation of being a jealous husband, if that's what's in your mind."

"But this is impossible!" Pettigrew protested. "Jack had spent the night at Sallowcombe in bed with his own wife. He can't have gone straight on to Highbarn and . . . "

"It doesn't seem probable, even for a man with Jack's reputation, does it, sir? All the same, if I was in charge of this case, I should make a few enquiries at

Highbarn. Whether I shall persuade Mr. Parkinson to, is another matter. He is very thorough, but rather slow in accepting suggestions. The trouble I had in getting him to send Jack's coat to the Forensic Science Laboratory you wouldn't believe."

"We seem to have moved on from *How?* to *By Whom?*" said Pettigrew. "I shouldn't have said that Tom was a murderous type myself, but then so few murderers are in my experience. What about Dick? After all, he was the man who really stood to profit by Jack's death—and still does, unless the unborn baby proves to be a boy."

Mallett shook his head.

"If Dick did it, I'm a Dutchman," he said. "I told you Tom was secretive, but Dick is just the opposite, with everything on the surface and ready to say the first thing that comes into his head—just as he did at the inquest. He might kill a man in hot blood—as any of us might—but he couldn't take a calculated risk. He couldn't have come along to me and asked me to help him prove that Jack died before Gilbert, knowing all the time that I only had to prove a little too much for him to be charged with murder. He just hasn't got it in him."

"And so we come back to Mr. Joliffe," said Pettigrew. "I should be so much happier if he could be cast as the villain of the piece throughout. I've taken a thorough dislike to him."

"But logically that's impossible, sir. Let me explain——"

"Don't bother. We've been over all the ground already, and I realize that it's only wishful thinking on

172

my part. I'm hopelessly prejudiced against the man anyway. Don't forget that he gave me the most unpleasant experience of my life at Bolter's Tussock last September. That reminds me of something I'd been meaning to ask you for some time. When Joliffe took the body out of his cold store on Tuesday morning, why did he go to the trouble of carting it back to Bolter's Tussock? There must have been scores of places just as good for his purposes and far more accessible to his shop at Whitsea."

"That point puzzled me too, sir. But I think there's no doubt that you were responsible for that."

"I was? In heaven's name, why?"

"Well, it so happens that Mr. Percy—you'll remember Mr. Percy, sir?"

"Percy Percy! I'll remember him to my dying day, I should think."

"Mr. Percy has a small farm on the other side of the moor and on the Monday, when his shop was closed, Joliffe went over to see him about some beasts he had to sell. They got talking of this and that, and Mr. Percy happened to mention——"

"That he had met a lunatic on Bolter's Tussock who claimed to have seen a dead body there. I can hear him saying it."

"Quite so, sir. Well, that must have put Joliffe in rather a difficulty. He wasn't to know that you had not been able to have a good look at this body so as to be able to give a clear description of it. He expected you to go off to the police with that description as soon as you could get out of bed."

173

Pettigrew cleared his throat self-consciously. "Quite so. Go on," he said.

"As I see it, he decided that it would be rather awkward if the police were told that Jack had been found on Bolter's Tussock on Saturday when they had found him miles away on Tuesday. They might go and look at Bolter's Tussock to make sure, and find something—bloodstains perhaps, or a button off his coat. Then they would start making the sort of enquiries which, in the end, I made. But if they found him on Bolter's Tussock on Tuesday *before* you had made any report to them——"

"—they would conclude that I was one of the imbeciles who always come forward to distract the police with imaginary stories as soon as they read about anything of this kind in the papers. Really, Mr. Mallett, there is something rather diabolical about this man Joliffe. Is there any good thing to be said about him?"

"Well, sir, to give him his due, I think he is really devoted to his little granddaughters. As Mrs. Gorman said in court, the whole of this business was devised to get the inheritance for them. I think the bitterest blow for him must be that as soon as she tumbled to what he had done she left him and took the children with her. One could almost feel sorry for him over that. He's a very lonely man just now."

"I refuse to pity him. Isn't he courting Louisa Gorman at Minster Tracy? She must be a lonely woman. They can console each other."

"No, sir. You're forgetting what Miss Greenway told

174

us this afternoon. That affair seems to have fizzled out now."

For a time it seemed that the conversation also had fizzled out. In the silence that followed Pettigrew jettisoned the butt of his cigar, and recharged Mallett's glass and his own.

"Aren't we running our heads against a brick wall?" he said at last. "Doesn't all the evidence point to accidental death?"

"I won't settle for accident until I can be sure of the kind of accident it was," said Mallett stubbornly. "And there's another thing, Mr. Pettigrew. This accident happened a deal too conveniently to satisfy me. He had only to live one day more for his daughters to come into all Gilbert's money. Don't tell me it was coincidence that he died when he did."

In that moment revelation came to Francis Pettigrew.

"Of course not!" he said. "You are perfectly right— it wasn't coincidence at all. I can see the whole thing now. Our whole trouble has been that we've been looking at this case from the wrong end. Look at it from the proper end and it sticks out a mile. Don't you see, Mallett? The reason why we haven't got the right answer is that *we've never asked the right question!*"

And he proceeded to ask the right question and to supply the answer to it with emphasis and elaboration.

Mallett had never been an emotional man—members of his profession cannot afford to be—and with increasing age his manner had become calmer and quieter than ever. He listened to Pettigrew's excited harangue with an air of no more than interested attention. When it was over he took time to refill and light his pipe. Then he said:

"You know, Mr. Pettigrew, I shouldn't be at all surprised if you were right. In fact, I think I'd be prepared to go so far as to say outright that you are right. As you say, once you look at the case from the proper angle all the probabilities point that way. It's a pity that we shall never be able to prove it, but at least you have the satisfaction of knowing the answer."

"Don't be so dismal," said Pettigrew. "In any case, it's not for us to prove anything. That's up to Parkinson and his merry men."

"Suppose I can persuade Mr. Parkinson to start this enquiry all over again from a new standpoint, do you suppose there'll be any evidence left after all this time?"

"Nobody can tell that till the evidence is looked for. There are some kinds of evidence that are indestructible. With any luck this will be."

"Let's hope so. I've got to persuade Inspector Parkinson, and Parkinson's got to persuade his Chief. Then if the preliminary enquiries indicate that we're on the right track, the Chief's got to persuade the Home Office. It will all take time, and the first stage will be the longest, I fancy. If there's nothing to show at the end of it, my name will be mud." He drained his glass and stood up. "And now if you'll excuse me, Mr. Pettigrew, I think it is time I went to bed. It has been a most rewarding evening and I'm very grateful to you for all you've done. If only——"

The Right Question

"Yes?"

"If only I could get an answer to that other problem that was troubling us, then I should really know we were on the right lines."

"I'm in a generous mood," said Pettigrew. "I'll answer that one for you too. Or rather, I'll tell you where to find the answer. It's in your library. *The Adventures of Sherlock Holmes*—or is it *The Memoirs*? Look it up when you get home—you'll recognise it easily enough."

"Sherlock Holmes," repeated Mallett. "I won't forget. Good night, sir, and thank you."

CHAPTER XVII

The Right Answer

About the middle of June, Pettigrew received a letter from Exmoor:

"Dear Mr. Pettigrew,

I thought you would be interested to know—the baby was born yesterday, and it's a boy. Dick Gorman rang me up to tell me, and I'm glad to say he's taken the news very well. I have Doreen and Beryl staying at Sunbeam while their mother is in hospital—did I tell you, my housekeeper was stepsister to Bob Gorman, Jack's third cousin, who lives at Combe Martin, so she is really one of the family?—and they are thrilled at having a brother. I expect they will be here another two or three weeks, when they will go to join their mother at Tracy Grange. It would give me very great pleasure if you and your good lady could come to spend a week here next month, after they have gone. The country should be looking very pretty then, and with no hunting going on, there won't be so many visitors about. I may say I have at last persuaded Mr. Parkinson to look into the matters we discussed the last time we met, and there may

be some interesting developments shortly. Looking
forward to seeing you,

I am,

Yours respectfully,

J. Mallett.

PS. I have looked up the Sherlock Holmes story you
were thinking of. I am sure you are right, but it seems to
be altogether too late to do anything about that now."

Owing to various difficulties and delays, it was not
until nearly the end of July that the Pettigrews were
able to accept Mallett's invitation. On the evening of
their arrival, they found him in his sitting-room
contemplating three silver porringers, four silver mugs
and half a dozen spoons of different shapes and sizes,
alike only in their emphatic ugliness.

"It's the christening to-morrow," he explained. "Mrs.
Gorman's asked me to be a godfather. Odd, isn't it,
considering that I nearly disinherited her, but she said
that if it hadn't been for me she would never have
known the truth about Jack, and by way of showing
her gratitude she'd like to make me responsible for his
son. Can you understand how women's minds work,
Mrs. Pettigrew?"

Eleanor, contemplating the fearsome array of silver,
murmured that she found men's minds also a little
difficult to understand sometimes.

"I wish you'd help me, ma'am," said Mallett. "I've
been so busy with other things that the matter of a
present went clean out of my mind, and I got these
in on appro at the last moment. Which shall I have?"

The Right Answer

Tactfully Eleanor steered Mallett's choice in the direction of the plainest and least offensive of the mugs, and then they became free to talk of other things.

The christening was fixed for half-past three, with tea at the Grange to follow. Mallett was taking his housekeeper to the service and proposed that his guests should accompany them. Pettigrew was quite prepared to go, but Eleanor, unhappy in the knowledge that her holiday clothes would not stand up to the full finery of the Gorman clan on a state occasion, protested vigorously that outsiders would not be welcome. Eventually it was arranged by way of a compromise that they should accompany Mallett to Minster Tracy, but spend the afternoon with Hester Greenway, who was only too glad to entertain them.

It was a fine day, and the prospective godfather was in high spirits, until something occurred on the way that seriously discomposed him. As they turned off the high road into the Minster Tracy lane, another car, coming in the opposite direction, turned also and followed them down the lane. Mallett, normally a punctiliously courteous driver, pulled up abruptly where the road was at its narrowest, so that the following car had to stop also. Then he got out and went back to speak to the other driver.

He was gone some time, and when he returned it was apparent that he was, for him, in a very bad temper.

"That idiot Parkinson!" he confided to Pettigrew, who was in the seat beside him. "For months now I've been on at him to get something done, and he has to choose to-day of all days!"

Pettigrew could think of nothing useful to say, and accordingly said nothing. Presently Mallett's sense of justice asserted itself.

"Of course, he wasn't to know," he went on. "And he says it's too late to stop anything now. He's promised to keep everyone out of the way as much as possible till the service is over, so I dare say it will be all right. But it is awkward, all the same. It's my godson I'm thinking of. Are babies of that age easily upset, do you think, Mr. Pettigrew?"

Pettigrew assured him that according to his experience, babies of that age were not normally upset by the activities of the police, and Mallett regained his calm. By the time they reached their destination, the police car had dropped behind and was nowhere to be seen.

It was evident when they arrived that the second smallest church in England was going to be fairly crowded that afternoon. Several cars were already drawn up along the road, and Mallett had to go some little distance to find a parking place. Hester Greenway was in position opposite the lych gate, watching the gathering of the clans with unabashed curiosity, and Frank and Eleanor joined her while the others went into the church.

"It's a wonderful turn-out," she told them. "I really think there are more Gormans here than at the last two funerals. Dick has come, with his wife and both the boys, which I think is rather noble of them, considering.

Unless the boys mean to try and drown the baby in the font—he has to live till he's twelve to make things safe for his mother, doesn't he?"

Another car drew up. From it alighted a plump young woman in a black skirt that fitted rather too tightly over her haunches.

"Ethel," murmured Hester, as they watched her hobble uncertainly towards the church door on her high heels. "Why Tom lets her walk about looking like that, I can't think. Where is Tom, I wonder? Surely he can't have decided to give the party a miss?"

Even as she spoke, a clatter of hooves made them look round. Tom was trotting up the lane on a thick-set dun cob that seemed familiar to Pettigrew. He waved to them cheerfully as he dismounted.

"I had to take the old horse to be shod this afternoon," he explained. "There was no time to get home afterwards, so I brought him straight on. Stand there!"

He walked through the lych gate, leaving the animal standing outside, its ugly, intelligent face looking over the churchyard wall in the direction in which its master had disappeared. Apart from an occasional flick of its tail to dislodge the flies, it stood as quiet and still as the tombstones themselves.

"What I wouldn't give for a beast like that!" Hester murmured enviously. "How did Tom train it, do you suppose? It's not a bit like his other cattle."

Hard behind Tom came the party from the Grange, in all the glory of a hired limousine with a uniformed chauffeur. The baby was almost invisible in an elaborate christening robe that must have done duty for generations of infant Gormans, but he and his mother were both eclipsed by the majestic presence of Louisa, splendid in black silk.

"Well!" said Hester, as the little procession, with Doreen and Beryl at its tail, filed into church. "That's another hatchet buried, it seems. What next, I wonder?"

It was a rhetorical question, but one to which Pettigrew was longing to have an answer. Some way up the lane to his left, he had noticed a car drawn into the side under the hedge, well away from those of the guests at the christening. Now out of the tail of his eye he could see that two or three men were following the perimeter of the churchyard, moving eastwards, away from where they stood. Their heads just shewed above the wall, and presently the church cut them off by view. Evidently Inspector Parkinson was doing his best to keep his word, but, as Mallett had said, it was awkward.

Pettigrew had no desire to add to the awkwardness. "Shall we be going?" he suggested. "I think we have seen all there is to see."

They turned to walk away, but had only taken a few steps when by common consent they halted.

Someone was coming up the lane towards them, a stoutish, pallid man, round-shouldered and unshaven, moving heavily and uncertainly. From his gait and from the state of his shoes it looked as though he had walked some way. In one hand he carried, incongruously enough, an enormous sheaf of scarlet gladioli. It was not until he was quite near to them that Pettigrew recognized Mr. Joliffe.

Joliffe was the first to speak.

183

The Right Answer

"Why, it's Mr. and Mrs. Pettigrew!" he said, in a voice that suggested he had been drinking. "This is a surprise! And Miss Greenway, too—I might have known you wouldn't be far away on such an occasion."

"Have you come for the christening?" Hester asked incredulously.

"Yes. I'm late, I know. I ran out of petrol down the road. Forgot to fill the tank—I forget things very, very easily nowadays, ever since—you know." He looked from one to another of them out of red-rimmed eyes. "And it needn't ever have happened—any of it—if I'd only known. That's the—what d'you call it?—*irony*, that's the word, the irony of the situation. My grandson! I'm entitled to come to his christening, aren't I?"

He took off his hat with a gesture. "Good-bye. Glad to have met you," he said, and walked past them through the lych gate, and up the path towards the church door.

Pettigrew contrived to get there before him.

"Mr. Joliffe," he said. "The service must be nearly over, and they'll all be coming out in a minute. Don't you think it would be better to wait outside instead of going in now and disturbing them?"

To his relief, Mr. Joliffe accepted the suggestion quite meekly.

"Good idea," he said. "I don't want to disturb anyone. All I do want is to see the little chap, and his mother. And the girls of course. They used to be fond of their old granddad. But it's my daughter I want the most, Mr. Pettigrew. It's her I brought these flowers for"—the gladioli trembled in his hand—"my own daughter!"

184

The Right Answer

Mr. Joliffe was lachrymose, pathetic and quite horrible. Pettigrew averted his eyes. A moment later the church door opened and the christening party poured out into the sunlight.

What happened next was in the nature of an anticlimax. For some time nobody noticed the presence of Mr. Joliffe at all. A cheerful throng of bonhomous Gormans elbowed him to one side while everyone took photographs of nearly everyone else. The mother, the godparents, the parson, Louisa, Doreen and Beryl were posed in varying permutations and combinations. The baby itself passed from one set of arms to another like the ball travelling down a line of three-quarters at Twickenham. It was Doreen who interrupted the orgy of photography by suddenly exclaiming, "Mum! There's grandpa!"

Edna Gorman was being photographed at the moment, with her son in her arms. She broke her pose at once, handed the infant to Louisa, who was standing near her, and went straight towards her father. The clamour of laughter and chat that had been filling the air was suddenly stilled, and the two met in utter silence.

"Edna, my dear, forgive me," said Joliffe. "But I had to come. These—these are for you, my dear."

With a clumsy gesture he thrust the flowers at his daughter. She stood motionless, looking at him as though at a stranger, making no move to take them.

"Take them, please!" he pleaded. "I meant all for the best, I did indeed."

With a sudden movement she snatched them from him. "Thank you, father," she said, in a small hard voice. "I wanted some flowers for Jack's grave. These will do very well."

She turned abruptly and walked down the side of the church towards the further end of the churchyard. Mallett, who had been in the background, a silent spectator, came suddenly to life. "Not that way, Mrs. Gorman!" he called. "Not that way! Stop her, some-one!" But it was too late. She had gone, and her father, still pleading and protesting, with her.

An ancient yew tree, marking no doubt what had formerly been the boundary of the graveyard, stood on the south side of the little church, level with its east end. Its branches now extended almost to the church walls, and tree and church between them effectively screened from sight the end of the churchyard where the most recent graves had been dug. Edna Gorman and her father came down the path between tree and church and stopped aghast. Between them and their objective a rough canvas barrier had been erected. A group of men, some in police uniform, were standing talking beside it. A little to one side, two others were leaning on spades, awaiting orders. As the purport of what she saw dawned upon her, Mrs. Gorman opened her mouth to scream, but no sound came. The flowers dropped from her hand, and Mallett was just in time to catch her as she fell.

Pettigrew was close behind Mallett. As he went forward to help he saw Joliffe coming back towards him, his face distorted with fear. He dodged past Pettigrew, and shambled rather than ran back along the way he had come to the west end of the church, into and through the group of men and women assembled there and on towards the lych gate. It was Tom Gorman who started the chase. "Tally-ho, boys! After him!" he cried, and Joliffe dashed into the lane with half the Gorman family in pursuit, hallooing and shouting, running after him because he was running away, they knew not why.

Joliffe took a despairing look over his shoulder. They were gaining on him, and there was no escape. Then, as he ran alongside the churchyard wall, he came abreast of Tom's horse, standing where it had been told to stand, its ears cocked, its nostrils quivering with excitement. In desperation he reached up for the reins and tried to put his foot in the stirrup. Tom shouted a warning, but it was unheard. In an instant the dun horse whipped round, tore the reins from Joliffe's grasp with a toss of its head, and, rearing on its hind legs, struck him two appalling blows full upon the chest with its new-shod fore-feet.

"*Silver Blaze*," said Mallett to Pettigrew some time later. "As you said, the answer was in my library all the time. It's one of my favourite Holmes stories, too. I should have guessed it."

"You hadn't my advantages," said Pettigrew. "I had seen this horse in action at Bolter's Tussock and knew what he was capable of. I suppose Jack tried to sneak off on him while his master was harbouring a stag in Satcherley Copse, and paid the penalty."

"Yes. Tom tells me that he found the body when he came back to where he had left his horse and decided that the easiest course was to say nothing about it. I have told him how foolish he has been——"

"Say no more, I beg. I have a strong fellow feeling for Tom in that respect. And after all, he was not to know that the animal was going to give a public demonstration of its lethal properties."

"But I don't understand," said Eleanor. "Why was Mr. Joliffe running away?"

"If you have murdered a man and seen him comfortably buried, it's only natural to run away when you find the police are digging him up again."

"But Jack wasn't murdered."

"No. But Gilbert was."

"*Gilbert?*"

"It's obvious when you come to think about it, isn't it? Only nobody ever did think about it. Joliffe had to ensure that Jack's death should seem to occur after Gilbert's. So he postponed the apparent date of Jack's decease, but he could only do that up to Tuesday morning, when his butcher's shop would reopen for business. There was a fair chance that Gilbert would be dead by then, but he couldn't be sure—so he made sure."

Hester could not contain her excitement.

"Ellie!" she exclaimed. "When we met him on that famous Saturday he had come straight from seeing Gilbert at the Grange. He said so himself."

"Exactly," said Pettigrew. "He was quite open about it—he could afford to be. He was paying a charitable call on his kinsman by marriage whom everybody knew to be dying of an incurable disease. What more natural than that in the course of his call he should give the sufferer a glass of water—and who was to know that there was anything in it besides water?"

The Right Answer

"What was in it?" Hester asked.

Mallett supplied the answer. "So far as my enquiries go," he said, "Joliffe on Saturday morning went to the chemist and bought a bottle of calomel—perfectly harmless to the ordinary man, but fatal to a patient in the last stages of kidney disease—or so the doctor tells me. Calomel, of course, contains mercury, and if that is what he used, the mercury could be traced in Gilbert's body easily enough. Parkinson will tell me when the pathologist makes his report, but I think that explains why Joliffe ran away."

"And he had only to leave things alone for nine months for everything to turn out as he desired," said Eleanor. "What was his expression? 'The *irony* of the situation'! "

At the end of their stay at Sunbeam Cottage, Eleanor and Frank made an early start on their way home. As they drove across Bolter's Tussock the morning mists were just clearing in prospect of a fine day. Opposite the place where Jack Gorman's body had lain Eleanor stopped the car and they walked out together on to the moor. A tall stag, his antlers still in velvet, rose from his couch in the heather and trotted quietly away. A curlew called unseen from the clouds close above their heads. The Ling Water babbled its quiet song from the valley below. It was entirely peaceful. The ghosts were gone from Bolter's Tussock.

CPSIA information can be obtained
at www.ICGtesting.com
Printed in the USA
BVHW050921100223
658271BV00003B/152